THE
MOMENT
Keeper

Available by
Buffy Andrews

THE MOMENT Keeper

Buffy Andrews

CARINA™

This edition is published by arrangement with Harlequin Books S.A. CARINA is a trademark of Harlequin Enterprises Limited, used under licence.

Published in Great Britain 2015
by CARINA, an imprint of Harlequin (UK) Limited,
Eton House, 18-24 Paradise Road,
Richmond, Surrey, TW9 1SR

© 2013 Buffy Andrews

ISBN 978-0-263-91775-8

98-0515

Harlequin (UK) Limited's policy is to use papers that are natural, renewable and recyclable products and made from wood grown in sustainable forests. The logging and manufacturing processes conform to the legal environmental regulations of the country of origin.

Buffy Andrews is an author, blogger, journalist and social media maven. Oh—and wife, mother, sister and friend.

By day she's a journalist, leading an award-winning staff at the *York Daily Record/Sunday News*, where she is Assistant Managing Editor of Features and Niche Publications and social media coordinator.

You will find her on a plethora of social networking sites, from Twitter and Facebook to RebelMouse and NewHive. She loves social media and loves to connect with her readers via the various platforms.

In addition to her writing blog, Buffy's Write Zone, she maintains a social media blog, Buffy's World.

She is also a newspaper and magazine columnist and writes middle-grade, young adult and women's fiction.

She loves hats and everything Disney. Her favourite colours are lime green and pink. She hates odd numbers and arrogant people. And if you ask her what her favourite book as a child was, she'll tell you *The Little House* by Virginia Lee Burton.

She lives in south central Pennsylvania with her husband, Tom; two sons, Zach and Micah; and wheaten cairn terrier Kakita. She is grateful for their love and support and for reminding her of what's most important in life.

Once you get to know Buffy, you will quickly see that she is a big believer in giving back. She has designated that five per cent of the proceeds from her books (eBook and print) will be given to charity. So when you buy her books, you help others.

In memory of Wendy,
who always believed.

CHAPTER 1

"But you promised. You promised you'd be there for me," says Olivia, tears exploding from her swollen eyes.

Cole runs his fingers through his dark, curly hair. "I know what I said. But. It's just that I'm supposed to go to college and…"

"So college is more important than me?"

"I didn't say that."

"You didn't have to."

"Look, Lib. I love you. You know that. I'm just not ready for this."

"And I am?"

"I didn't mean it like that. We're both not ready."

"Well, it's a little too late for that realization. You should have thought about that two months ago when you convinced me to have sex with you."

Cole punches the bed and stands up. "Damn it, Lib. That's a cheap shot. You're not going to pin this all on me. You wanted to do it, too. It's not like I forced you."

"Just leave. Leave."

"I don't want to leave you like this. I want to talk about our options."

"Options? There are no options. I'm pregnant. With your child. You don't want it. You've made that clear. Look, this is my problem. Not yours. So just go. Now."

Cole grabs his varsity jacket and takes two steps toward Olivia before she backs away. "Look, Lib. I can't talk to you when you get like this. Can we talk later? When you calm down."

"There's nothing to talk about. We did it once. Once. And I got pregnant and you want out. Well, I'm giving you your out. There's the door."

"Lib, if I could go back in time and change that one moment I would." Cole walks out the bedroom door and Olivia throws one of Daisy's squeaky toys at him. The rubber bone hits Cole in the back but he doesn't turn around.

Olivia flops on her bed and pulls her boney knees up to her heaving chest. Tears soak her blue satin pillow. Her cries feel like a knife twisting in my heart. I want to comfort her. To hold her in my arms and tell her that things are never as bad as they seem. That I understand her pain and that she needs to be strong.

But I can't.

All I can do, all I have ever been able to do, is watch and record the moments of her life as they unfold. I'm her moment keeper. It's my job to record her life story, to capture and hold every moment she ever lived so that when she dies I'm able to play them back for her, one after another.

Olivia spots her purple fuzzy bathrobe draped over the footboard of her cherry bed. She pulls the belt out and sits up, wrapping it around her right hand. I know what she's thinking. I always know. It's part of being her moment keeper. I always know what she thinks and feel what she feels. Her joys and sorrows and fears become mine.

Of all of the moments I've recorded in Olivia's life, this is the most difficult yet. She's thinking about killing herself, about using her bathrobe belt, wondering if it's strong enough or if she should use one of the leather belts in her closet.

It takes me back to the day my life ended – the day I killed myself.

* * *

The moment I pulled the trigger, I knew it was a mistake. But it was too late. I was dead and there was no turning back.

I had thought about the moment forever. Pictured it in my mind again and again. Like it was some damn movie that never ended. Just played over and over and over.

I thudded to the floor, sinking in a pool of blood. Someone reached for my hand and told me to come. She wasn't talking talking but thinking what she wanted me to hear. Her name was Wendy and she knew that my name was Sarah.

She was iridescent and flowing and not well defined. Sort of shaped like a person but not quite. More like a ghost. Don't ask me how, but I knew she was friendly. I knew that she wanted to help me.

She was pulling me, pulling me. But it wasn't me, me. That me was bathed in blood on the cold bathroom floor where I shot myself just seconds before.

We flowed away from the blood-splattered bathroom toward a vertical thin line of light. Wendy told me I had a job to do. Job to do? I almost laughed. Can a dead person laugh? Maybe not quite.

I heard voices and looked back. The Ace of Hearts Grandma gave me floated in the expanding pool of blood.

I felt Wendy tug and I turned to see the vertical thin line of light widen and suck us in like a strong vacuum before sealing completely.

I was surrounded by hundreds of iridescent beings and then I realized that I was one, too. We stood, er, floated in the middle, surrounded by all of these beings or spirits or whatever they were. Wendy put her hands on my head and held them there.

A tingling coursed through me as I heard Wendy in my mind. She explained that I, like her, was a moment keeper. She told me that she would show me the moments of my life, moments she had collected since my birth.

What I saw brought me great pain and joy. There were days upon days spent in Grandma's arms or by her side. And days upon days of my dad coming home smelling like he'd bathed in whiskey. I begged Wendy to stop when a moment was too painful, but she just kept going. I began to see how one moment was tied to another and another and how they intertwined to form the tapestry of my life, a life that ended much too soon at my own hands.

Wendy said it was my turn to be a moment keeper, my turn to record the moments in someone's life just as she had recorded those in mine. She was moving on to a place where time didn't exist, a place where only happy moments were allowed and the bad ones were left behind.

I pleaded with Wendy to stay, to help me. How was I to know how to do this moment-keeper thing? What if I screwed it up? Missed recording a memory? But she just wrapped me in her warmth and somehow I knew I would be all right. She had given me one last gift – the confidence and understanding I needed to do what I had to do. And when she released me from her embrace, she was gone and I was on earth beside Olivia.

CHAPTER 2

"Oh, Tom, isn't she the most beautiful baby you've ever seen? Perfect in every way."

Tears pull in Elizabeth's chocolate eyes as she kisses the head of the sleeping infant in her arms.

Tom sits down beside her on the burgundy leather couch. "So what do you want to name her? How about Hope because she's everything that we had hoped for?"

Elizabeth looks up at Tom. "Can we give her my grandmother's name? And Hope for her middle name?"

"So Olivia Hope?"

Elizabeth nods.

"That's perfect," Tom says. "Olivia Hope Kennedy."

* * *

Watching this tender moment made me feel warm. That's what happens when a moment keeper records a good moment, a happy one. Our spirit bodies feel warm. We can't cry or turn red or show any of the outward physical signs a living human would, but warmth courses through our spirit bodies when a moment is joyful and a razor-sharp chill when it's not.

I felt jealous while I was recording this moment for Olivia. The day I was named was painful to watch when Wendy had shown it to me.

"Christ, Mom. I don't know how to care for a baby."

"Matt, I'll help you. But I'm begging you to get help. I know that you're angry."

"Damn right I'm angry. Sue should be here. Not her."

"Going through with the pregnancy was Sue's decision. It's what she wanted."

"Yeah, and it killed her."

"You need to give her a name, Matt."

"You name her. I gotta get out of here, Mom."

"Matt, stay away from that bar. You're drinking too much."

"No, I'm not drinking enough!"

I watched as Matt left, slamming the door behind him. Grandma cradled me in her thick arms and sang me a sweet lullaby. She kissed my forehead and named me Sarah, after her favorite woman of the Bible. "It means princess," she said, "and that's what you are. Grandma's little princess."

I always thought Matt resented me, but I never knew why. I knew my mom had died in childbirth, but I never knew from what. Grandma, who raised me, never wanted to talk about it. And Matt, well, let's just say he wasn't in the running for Father of the Year Award. He spent most of his time on a bar stool at the local watering hole around the corner from our house. His drinking got so bad that Grandma eventually kicked him out and she became my legal guardian. The day I became Grandma's was the happiest day of my life. Ever. I finally belonged to someone who loved me, really loved me.

* * *

"Oh, Tom!" Elizabeth says. "Not another one. You're going to spoil her. We've only had her for three days and you've already brought home four stuffed animals."

Tom picks up Olivia. "How's Daddy's little girl today?" and kisses her chubby pink cheek. "Tell Mommy that daddies are supposed to spoil their little girls."

Elizabeth walks over, bags under her eyes and hair thrown back in a lopsided ponytail. She puts her arms around Tom and Olivia.

"How was your day, Liz?" Tom asks.

"Despite not getting enough sleep and hanging in my pajamas most of the day because I didn't have the energy to shower, I'd say things are going pretty well."

"It'll get better," Tom says. "Every new parent feels the way you do."

"I know," Elizabeth says. "Don't get me wrong, I'm happy that we have the family we've always wanted. Just happened so fast and I wasn't as prepared as I thought I'd be."

"You're doing just fine, Liz. Don't beat yourself up."

"But I want to do everything right for her. I want to be the best mommy I can."

"And you are," Tom says. "You love her. That's what's most important."

Tom kisses Elizabeth on her forehead and she leaves to order pizza — the night before it was Chinese — because she's too tired to cook. Tom rocks Olivia and tells her about his day in the ER.

"And then Daddy had to stitch a woman's hand because she cut it while slicing a bagel. And next, a mommy brought in a little boy who had swallowed a tiny Lego piece he had found while crawling on the floor. And that was Daddy's day, Libby Love."

And he kisses her forehead and places his index finger onto her tiny palm. Olivia's fingers curl around his, hugging it so tightly her knuckles turn white.

* * *

So Olivia's dad's a doctor. I had learned while recording an earlier moment that her mom was a nurse. Reminded me of what a deadbeat dad I had. I tried to forget the day Matt lost his job, but Wendy's montage of my life included this moment.

"Just look at you," Grandma said. "You smell like the bottle and you look like an unmade bed. No wonder you lost your job, Matt. You've got to pull yourself together. No one's going to hire you looking like that."

Matt punched the brown frayed chair he stood next to. "Just take care of her. Don't worry about me."

I hadn't realized until I saw my life moments one after another how seldom, if ever, Matt referred to me by my name. I was always "she" or "her" or "the baby" or "that girl" or "that kid". There were very few times when he said "Sarah". I wondered if he avoided saying my name because it made me seem more human, more difficult to blame and hate. As he would any enemy, I think he preferred to keep me at a distance.

* * *

Elizabeth walks into the room. "You hold her so much you're going to spoil her," she tells Tom, who is still rocking Olivia.

Elizabeth walks over to Tom and lightly brushes Olivia's tiny head. She doesn't have much hair and what she does have is so light that she looks bald.

"I love watching her sleep," Tom says. "She looks so peaceful."

Elizabeth smiles. "Makes you wonder how something so beautiful can come out of so much ugliness."

* * *

Ugliness, I thought. You haven't seen ugly until you've seen Matt come home drunk and wreck our home.

"Matt, stop," Grandma yelled. "Stop or I'll call the police."

Matt just laughed and held a lamp in his hand. "You won't call the police. You never call the police," he said, his words slurring together so you couldn't tell where one stopped and the next one began.

Grandma carried me, then three, into her room and locked the door. I heard glass breaking and Matt cursing. I heard what sounded like furniture flipping over. Then I heard a knock on the door. It was the police.

I buried my head in Grandma's chest. I loved being so close to her heart. Its beating always soothed me. We watched as the police led Matt away. The house was a disaster. That was the beginning of the end. That was ugliness.

CHAPTER 3

"Wait until I tell Daddy that you got your first tooth," Elizabeth says as she changes Olivia's diaper. "And guess what today is? Your six-month birthday! That's half of a year."

Elizabeth pulls pink pants over Olivia's diaper then slips a pink top with brown polka dots over her tiny head. She picks up a basket filled with hair wear and slips a pink stretchy headband over Olivia's head, positioning the flower on the right side, toward the front. "You're getting so big. Yes, you are."

Elizabeth picks up Olivia and twirls her around, and Olivia giggles. Elizabeth stops and pulls Olivia into her chest and kisses her cheek.

"I love you so much, Princess Libby. You'll always be my princess, my little girl."

A tear slides down Elizabeth's cheek and her smile swallows her creamy face.

* * *

"Look, Matt," Grandma said as he walked into the kitchen.

I sat in the metal high chair giggling as Grandma pretended the spoon was an airplane and made airplane noises as she flew the spoon toward my mouth.

"Coming in for a landing," Grandma said. "Open wide."

I opened my mouth and Grandma slid the spoon in, scooping up the cereal that slid from my rubbery lips onto my chin.

Matt walked over. "What did you want to show me?"

"Sarah's got her first tooth. See it there? On the bottom? That little piece of white poking through her gum."

"Yeah, so what? She's got a damn tooth. I have a mouthful."

"Matt, it's your baby's first tooth."

"She's more your baby than mine," said Matt, pouring a cup of coffee and walking away.

He paused when he got to the door and turned around. "The tooth is nice."

* * *

"Where did you find that?" Elizabeth asks Tom as he walks in carrying a stuffed tooth about the size of a grapefruit.

"Where I buy all of her stuffed animals," he said.

"The store at the mall?"

Tom nodded. "They have everything there."

Elizabeth smiles. "Yeah, and pretty soon we'll have it all here."

"Gotta celebrate the milestone, Liz."

Tom shakes the fuzzy white tooth and it rattles. "Lookie what Daddy has, Libby Love."

He walks over to the playpen and picks up Olivia. He shakes the tooth and Olivia laughs. Slobber slides down her chin and onto her pink bib embroidered with "Daddy's little girl". Tom gives Olivia the rattle and she shakes it and giggles. As always, Elizabeth snaps photo after photo. Her camera and video recorder are never far from her.

* * *

"Where are you going?" Grandma asked Matt.

"Out."

"Out where?"

"Just Out."

"Matt, this has got to stop. Drinking every night. Your grandfather died a drunk and I swore I would never bring up a child in the same house as a drunk."

"I'm not a drunk. I just need to get away at night."

"Then go to the gym instead of that bar. It'd be better for you."

"My friends are at that bar."

"Friends? You call them friends?"

"Yeah. Friends."

"They're losers, Matt. A bunch of deadbeat dads and worthless husbands. If Sue were alive she'd…"

Matt whipped around. Fire-engine red flooded his scrappy unshaven face. He hammered the air with his arm, using the movement to emphasize his words. "Don't. You. Ever. And I mean never. Bring Sue up. She's gone. Died and left me with her."

He pointed to me in the playpen.

"Don't blame Sarah for Sue's death, Matt. That little girl is the best of both of you."

"Well, then take her. Celebrate her first tooth and leave me the hell out of it."

Matt walked out the door and Grandma picked me up and held me and cried me to sleep.

* * *

"Are you sure you want to go out tonight?" Elizabeth asks Tom.

"We haven't been out alone since we got Libby. As much as I love her, I want to take you on a special date. Don't worry. Your mom knows what to do."

Elizabeth hugs Olivia before putting her in the playpen so she can finish getting ready.

"Do you think I'm getting fat?" she asks Tom, turning around in the black silk dress she bought at the new boutique by the bank.

"Yeah, as a matter of fact I was just thinking how much you're starting to resemble a pregnant hippo." Tom laughs.

Elizabeth picks up the hairbrush on her vanity and throws it at him. "I'm serious. Do you think my butt's getting fat?"

"No, Liz. Your butt's beautiful."

"What about my thighs?"

"They're perfect, too."

"My boobs?"

"Not that I wouldn't mind it if they were fatter, er, bigger, but they're the same size they've always been. And they're perfect."

"There has to be some part of me that's not beautiful or perfect," Elizabeth says.

"Well, now that you mention it, you do have a little wiry hair that grows out of that mole beside your lip that looks a little witchy. Sometimes, I just want to pluck it but I'm too scared to touch it. I think it might attack me."

Elizabeth chases Tom around the room and wrestles him to the ground and Libby starts to cry.

"You're making her cry," Tom says.

The bell rings.

"Lucky for you, Mom's here," Elizabeth says.

Tom opens the door and Cindy walks in carrying her bag of knitting supplies.

"There's my little princess," she says, putting her bag on the antique cherry table.

She takes Olivia from Tom. "It's just me and you tonight, my little Libby Love."

Elizabeth walks into the room wearing her new dress that showcases her hourglass figure and endless toothpick legs.

Tom whistles.

Cindy smiles. "You look like a million bucks, Liz."

"Thanks, Mom. Are you sure you know what to do?"

"Liz. I had five daughters. I think I know what to do. Quit worrying. Go out with your husband and have some fun. Just because you're parents doesn't mean you stop being a couple."

"I know, but..."

"But nothing. Libby and I will be fine. Now go."

Elizabeth sees the knitting bag on the table. "What are you making now?"

"Oh, just another sweater for Libby."

"But you already made her two."

"Well, I decided she needed another one. This one's a pretty green. Oh, and I'm also knitting her some hats. Found a pattern with this cute flower in the front that I think she'll look adorable in."

Elizabeth smiles and kisses Libby then her mom. "Thanks, Mom. You're the best."

She takes a couple of steps then turns around. "Mom, is there a hair coming out of this mole beside my mouth?"

Elizabeth sticks out her head and tilts her chin so her mom can examine the mole.

"I don't see any hair. Who said you had a hair? Did you see a hair?"

Tom laughs and Cindy looks at him. "Don't tell my daughter she has a hair coming out of her mole because we will never hear the end of it. Now go and have some fun."

* * *

"Which one do you like better?" Grandma asked me. "The pink or the purple?"

A baby me sat in the seat of the blue plastic shopping cart, looking at the two bolts of fabric in Grandma's hands.

"Ma. Ma. Ma."

"That's right. Grandma's right here. Would you like Grandma to make you a pink dress or a purple dress?"

"May I help you?" a saleswoman asked Grandma.

"Yes, please. I'll take this pink and purple, oh, and why not, that yellow."

Grandma pointed to the pale yellow fabric behind her. "I can't decide so I'll make her all three."

The saleswoman smiled at me. "She's an absolute doll. Is her hair naturally curly?"

"Yes, just like her mother's."

"You're a lucky little girl," the saleswoman said to me. "I wish I had someone to make me dresses."

The saleswoman got the fabric for Grandma and we headed for checkout.

"Next on our list, Sarah, is to get you a coat."

"Ma. Ma. Ma."

Grandma picked me up and put me in her dented Chevy sedan and we pulled out of the discount department store parking lot and headed for the Goodwill store.

CHAPTER 4

"That's it, Libby. Pull yourself up. Good girl. Now come to Daddy."

I watch as Tom coaxes Olivia, who's holding onto the edge of the cherry coffee table, to let go and walk toward him. Olivia smiles and giggles and lifts her pudgy, dimpled hands. She takes one step toward Tom before falling backward on her diaper-clad bottom.

She pulls herself up again and falls backward again. After a few more tries, Olivia takes two steps toward Tom before he catches her and keeps her from falling.

Tom continues to work with Olivia, moving farther and farther from her. She takes high marching steps, lifting her knees, then jabbing the floor with her tiny feet. Eventually, she toddles to Tom and falls into his open arms. She seems surprised that she was able to walk that far without falling. She giggles some more.

"Good girl, Libby. Good girl." He hugs her and kisses her freshly bathed head. "Wait until Mommy sees what we've been working on. She's going to be so proud of you."

Just yesterday, Olivia had pulled herself up and walked around the coffee table while holding onto it for the first time. Today, she finally gets the nerve to let go.

Tom scoops her up and sits on the couch and reads her a book before tucking her into bed.

* * *

I don't think Matt ever did anything with me. If he had loved me an eighth of what Tom loves Olivia, maybe things would have been different. But you can't make someone love you. Believe me, I tried. I tried to be good all of the time. Do everything I was told. But Matt was always so angry. Even when I learned to walk and Grandma was so proud of me the only thing on Matt's mind was how my newfound freedom made me even more of a pain in the ass.

"Can't you keep her in one room?" Matt asked Grandma one day.

"Matt, she's not an animal that you can cage. It's natural for her to want to explore."

"Well, I don't need her exploring and getting into my stuff."

"Then close your bedroom door. Besides, maybe she just wants to be near you."

"Well, I don't want to be near her. Keep her out of my room, out of my stuff."

"Why don't you just move out if you're that miserable?" Grandma said.

"Don't worry, when I can afford to I will."

* * *

Elizabeth holds up princess-themed party invitations. "How about this, Libby?"

Olivia sits in the grocery cart gnawing on a red plastic teething ring. Her yellow bib is soaked from her drool.

"Princess invitations for a princess," Elizabeth says as she puts them in the cart. "After all, you only turn one once."

Elizabeth finds the coordinating tableware and tosses plates, cups, napkins, tablecloths, a centerpiece, utensils, pink and white streamers and other party decorations into the cart. She then orders a balloon bouquet for the big day, selecting a huge princess balloon along with several Mylar balloons and a few latex ones.

"She's cute," the clerk tells Elizabeth.

"Thank you."

"Love her curly hair. Guess she gets that from her father."

Elizabeth, whose hair is straight as straw, smiles. "Actually, we're not sure where she gets it from."

"That's like me," the clerk says. "I was born without two adult teeth. My dentist said it's a congenital thing, usually hereditary. But Mom doesn't know anyone in the family who's missing two teeth."

"So what did you do?" Elizabeth asks.

"About what?"

"The teeth."

"Oh. Got implants, and they were way expensive. Mom said she's spent a mint on my mouth."

"Well, they look nice," Elizabeth says. "You have a great smile. I would never have known your teeth weren't real."

"Thanks."

Olivia's teething ring falls on the floor. Elizabeth picks it up and puts it in her purse and pulls out another one from the diaper bag to give her.

"I hope she's not missing any teeth," the clerk says.

Elizabeth smiles. "Me, too. I suppose we'll just have to wait and see. There's some things I guess you just don't know."

* * *

"Happy birthday to you. Happy birthday to you. Happy birthday dear Sarah. Happy birthday to you."

Grandma placed the cake she had baked in front of me. It had vanilla icing and she decorated it with sprinkles and a big candle in the shape of the numeral one. It was just me and Grandma. There were no aunts or uncles or cousins. Grandma had no family. And there was no Matt.

Grandma snapped photos as I dug my baby fingers into the cake.

"Taste the icing, Sarah," she said. "Mmm, good."

I started to tear up. Icing dripped from my hands. I didn't like being messy. Grandma took a swipe of the icing with her index finger and put it up to my mouth. I tasted the sweet icing and realized the stuff on my fingers was good. Real good. I licked the icing off my fingers and dug them back into the cake and licked them clean again and again.

Grandma laughed. "That's my girl. Get messy. Enjoy it. You're one."

I had cake and icing in my hair and all over my face. Grandma waited until I was good and messy and the cake was wrecked before removing it from the tray on my high chair.

* * *

"Do you ever think about her mother?" Elizabeth asks Tom.

"I try not to," Tom says. "I mean, I'm grateful we have Libby, but I don't understand how her mother could do what she did."

"Do you worry that we don't know anything about her mother?"

"Like what?"

"Oh, I don't know. Like if she was born without two adult teeth."

Tom tilts his head and scrunches his eyes so his eyebrows almost meet in the middle. "What are you talking about?"

Elizabeth shifts in her seat. "The clerk at the party store told me she was born without two adult teeth. Said it was congenital."

"So?"

"Well, it just got me thinking. We don't know the birth mother's health history. What if Libby's missing two of her adult teeth or…?"

"Look, Liz. We can't worry about what we don't know. If Libby is missing two adult teeth, then we'll get her two. Simple as that. Whatever Libby faces, we'll be there to help her. No matter what that might be."

"I love you," Elizabeth tells Tom. "Thanks for putting up with my worrying self."

Tom kisses her. "You wouldn't be you if you didn't worry. But worry about the things you can control, not the things you can't. Whatever happens, we're in this together."

* * *

"You missed your daughter's first birthday," Grandma told Matt as he stumbled into the kitchen. He popped a handful of aspirin into his mouth and chased them with a swig of black coffee.

"Sorry. I forgot."

"That collection department called again," Grandma said. "You better call them back."

Matt didn't answer.

"Have any interviews lined up?"

Matt shook his head.

"You need to find something, Matt. You've got bills to pay."

"Christ, Mom. Can't I just eat breakfast in peace for once?"

He looked at me in my high chair eating Cheerios.

"Da. Da." I pinched a Cheerio and offered it to him.

Matt's eyes became glassy. He held out his palm and I placed the Cheerio in it. His lips mashed into a limp smile, and he slid the Cheerio into his jeans pocket.

He didn't realize that Grandma was watching. She placed her hand over her heart and a tear slipped from the corner of her wrinkled eye.

Matt grunted goodbye and left, slamming the door behind him. He was gone. Again.

Grandma walked over to me and patted the top of my head. "There's a man who's spent so much time being angry that he doesn't know how to be anything but. Don't let anger consume you, Sarah. Anger destroys everything that's good."

CHAPTER 5

Elizabeth gathers silky strands of hair into a cluster on top of Olivia's head and clips it with a pink lacey bow. "Such a pretty girl."

"Da. Da. Da."

"Yes, Daddy is getting his picture taken, too."

Tom walks into the nursery, with a beautiful hand-painted mural depicting various nursery rhymes, and Olivia claps her pudgy hands. "Da. Da. Da."

He picks up Olivia and kisses her and then Elizabeth. "My girls look beautiful."

"Do you like our matching dresses?" Elizabeth asks.

Tom smiles. "Gorgeous, as always."

The dresses are a pink floral print. Elizabeth's is sleeveless and Olivia's has capped sleeves and a big bow around the waist that ties in the back.

"Found them online at a really neat boutique. Bought two others."

"Don't tell me anymore," Tom says. "I don't want to know how much this new online boutique is costing me."

Elizabeth tilts her head and fakes a pout. "You always say your girls deserve the best."

"Yep," Tom said. "Nothing but the best."

* * *

I remember the day I was cleaning out Grandma's closet. It was right after she died and I was making good on my promise to donate all of her clothes to Goodwill. I found a big box of pictures stuffed in a dark corner underneath a stack of old wool blankets. I spent the entire afternoon looking through them. There were photos of Matt when he was little. It was hard to believe that the freckled-faced boy with the toothless grin in the red and blue Spider-Man pajamas had become one of the biggest drunks on this side of the Mason-Dixon Line.

I found pictures of Matt's dad, my grandfather, who died from a heart attack when Matt was in ninth grade. That's when Matt met my mom. They sat beside one another in science class. Grandma told me the story. She said my mom grew up in foster homes and that my parents got married right out of high school. "Way too young," she said. "But you couldn't tell them any different."

I opened a small manila folder and found my parents' wedding pictures. It didn't look as if there were a lot of people at the wedding. Just Grandma and a couple of my parents' friends. Maybe a half-dozen people. It looked as if it was held in the white gazebo at the park by the high school. I recognized the gazebo's copper cupola with a finial on top and the brick walkway that circled the structure.

My parents looked so young in the pictures, Mom in her white cotton dress and Matt in a pair of black dress pants, white shirt and tie. The flowers Mom held looked like one of those cheap bouquets you can buy at the grocery store.

There were lots of pictures of me, a few of me and Grandma and none, not one, of me and Matt.

* * *

"I love this one," Elizabeth says when the photographer displays the photos she has just taken on the computer screen.

"Me, too," Tom says.

Olivia is sitting on a white rocker, holding a doll that's wearing a pink floral dress just like hers.

"You didn't tell me you got the doll a matching dress," Tom says.

Elizabeth smiles. "I couldn't resist. It was just too adorable."

They look at all of the pictures and purchase several poses of Olivia and several poses of all three of them.

"Remember our wedding pictures?" Elizabeth says.

"How could I forget? We had a best man, a maid of honor, six bridesmaids, six ushers, a flower girl and ring bearer and the photo session took forever."

"But we got great photos," Elizabeth said.

"Yeah, but I'm not sure our five hundred guests were happy that they had to wait so long."

"It wasn't five hundred, it was four hundred. And besides, the strolling musician and hors d'oeuvres held them over."

* * *

I had a doll with a matching dress once. I named her Sue, after my mom. It was Twins' Day in preschool and no one wanted to dress like me. Grandma made all of my clothes and, even though I thought they were beautiful, they didn't quite compare with the store-bought ones. Grandma thought the newer styles were too grown-up for a little girl just learning to print her name. So she used older patterns that she felt were more appropriate.

The teacher didn't know I didn't have a partner. She thought Marybeth was my partner. But Marybeth decided that she wanted to dress like Melissa and Kristin, who always wore the latest fashions. So instead of twins they were triplets. When I told Grandma that I didn't have a partner and that I didn't want to go to school that day, she said she would make a dress for my doll and that I could take her. So, that's what I did.

I loved that red dress with the white trim and big red bow and I loved that doll. Most of all, I loved Grandma.

* * *

"What's it now?" Tom asks.

"103. The pediatrician said there's a bug going around and that high fevers are a part of it."

"So she doesn't want to see her?"

"If Libby's not feeling better by tomorrow and she still has a high fever, the doctor said to bring her in."

"Do you want me to sleep in her room tonight?" Tom asks.

"No," Elizabeth says. "You have to get up for work tomorrow. Can you pump up the air mattress, though?"

Tom gets the air mattress from the basement and pumps it up while Elizabeth rocks Olivia and sings her a lullaby.

* * *

When I was sick, Grandma took care of me. She'd rock me and hold me and soothe me.

"It's OK, Sarah. It's OK," Grandma said as she tucked two-year-old me in her bed. "The medicine should work soon. Shh, baby girl. Shh."

Grandma crawled in bed beside me and wrapped her arm around me and pulled me closer. "These darn ear infections. Hopefully the surgery will help."

* * *

Tom peeks in the nursery. Olivia is asleep beside Elizabeth on the air mattress. "Liz," he whispers, trying not to wake up Olivia.

Elizabeth stirs.

"How's the fever? Do you need me to take off work?"

"No," Elizabeth says. "Fever finally broke."

"Well, if you need me, call me."

Elizabeth nods.

"I love you. Tell Libby I love her, too.'

* * *

"What do you mean she has to have surgery?" Matt asked Grandma.

"Just what I said. The poor child has had one ear infection after another. The doctor says she needs to have tubes put in her ears."

"And how am I supposed to pay for it?" Matt asks. "That lousy insurance I have won't begin to cover this."

"I worked out a payment plan with the doctor. I'll pick up a couple more houses to clean and any extra alteration work at the bridal shop. Can you get any more hours at the factory?"

"They're cutting back, not adding hours."

"Well, if you give me the money you spend on beer each week that would help."

"Don't start, Mom. It's only a couple of beers a week."

"It's more than a couple, Matt. Have you gone to any of those meetings yet?"

Matt pushed out his chair and threw down his paper napkin. "No, and I don't plan to either."

He left the house and it was just Grandma and me – again.

CHAPTER 6

Olivia points to the three stick figures on her drawing. "That's Daddy and Mommy and me."

Elizabeth picks up Olivia and hugs her. "I love your drawing. And I love that we're all smiling."

Olivia nods.

Elizabeth puts Olivia down. "Where should we put it?"

They search the stainless-steel refrigerator for some open space, but Olivia's artwork covers every inch of the appliance.

"How about in the office?" Elizabeth says.

Olivia follows Elizabeth into the office crowded with heavy oak furniture. The bulletin board behind the desk is covered with Olivia's artwork but Elizabeth makes room by overlapping some pieces and puts the new picture right in the middle.

"The perfect place for the perfect picture of the perfect family," Elizabeth says.

"Per-vect," Olivia says.

* * *

"I'd like you to draw a picture of your family," Miss Becky told the kindergarten class. "Afterward, you can share what you drew."

Miss Becky gave each of us a big sheet of white paper and a pack of new crayons. I ran my finger over the pointy crayon tips. My crayons at home had been worn down to stubs. I sat beside Reid and Rachel.

I drew a big circle for Grandma's head and a smaller one for mine. I glanced over at Reid's paper. He was drawing a lot of circles. Each one was connected to a stick body. The figures were different heights. I looked at Rachel's paper. She had drawn three stick figures and a flat circle with four stick legs coming out of the bottom.

I pointed to the flat circle. "What's that?"

Rachel looked up at me, her black licorice eyes swallowing her cornrow-framed face. "My dog."

"What's his name?" I asked.

"Peanut Butter."

Reid laughed.

Rachel covered her drawing with her arms.

"I like that name," I said.

Rachel pulled her paper toward me and shifted in her seat so her back was blocking Reid from seeing her picture.

"OK, children," Miss Becky said. "Time to share. Anyone want to volunteer to go first?"

Reid's hand shot up. He was always first to volunteer for anything.

"OK, Reid. Come to the front of the classroom so everyone can see your picture."

Reid pushed out his chair and walked to the front and stood next to Miss Becky.

"This is my dad and this is my mom," he said, pointing to the different stick figures on the big sheet of white paper. "And these are my sisters. Rebecca. Rachelle. Renee. And Randi. And that's me."

"So you have four sisters?" Miss Becky asked.

Reid shook his head so fast I thought his thick black glasses would fly off.

"And a cat but I forgot to drawn him. His name is Rudy."

"Very good," Miss Becky said.

"And guess what?" Reid asked. He didn't wait for Miss Becky to reply. "Our names all start with R."

"That's right," Miss Becky said. "They do."

Reid walked back to his seat, strutting like one of those Mummers Grandma always likes to watch on TV on Thanksgiving Day.

"Who would like to go next?"

I sat and listened as student after student talked about their families. I didn't want to share my drawing. But eventually I was the only one left who hadn't gone.

"Sarah," Miss Becky said. "Your turn."

I picked up my drawing and went to the front of the class. "This is me and my grandma."

Reid raised his hand.

"Yes, Reid," Miss Becky said.

"Where's your mom and dad?"

My body stiffened, like the time Grandma caught me sneaking chocolate-chip cookies after she said I couldn't have any more because we were soon going to eat dinner.

I swallowed hard. "I don't have any."

Reid tilted his head and even with his thick glasses on I could tell he was scrunching his beady little eyes. "Why not?"

"You know, Reid," Miss Becky interrupted. "Just like there are different kinds of ice cream, there are many different kinds of families. Some families have moms and dads and sisters and brothers. Others have just a mom or just a dad or a grandma or a grandpa. What's important to remember is that they are all families no matter how they are made up."

Reid scratched his head.

Rachel raised her hand.

"Yes, Rachel," Miss Becky said.

Rachel smiled. "I like Sarah's picture."

From that day on, Rach and I were inseparable.

* * *

"And God bless Mommy and Daddy," says Olivia, her fingers, stained with magic marker, interlocked and her eyes pinched shut. "And Emma and Jack. And the nice lady at the deli who gave me a slice of cheese. And the man who came to the house and gave Mommy flowers from Daddy. And my teacher, Mrs. Plato. And those people Mommy and I saw waiting for food outside that building on the way to school today. Oh, and God bless Pepper. That's our neighbor's cat. He has three legs. Amen."

"That was a very nice prayer," Elizabeth says, brushing Olivia's ringlets off her face.

Tom agrees. "I know who Emma is. Who's Jack?"

"He's new at school. I played with him today. He said he doesn't have a mommy or a daddy. He has a grandma."

Tom looked at Elizabeth. "Well, princess. I'm glad you played with Jack. I'm sure that made him feel good."

"Yeah. He cried. A lot. And then when we started to play, he stopped. For a little. But then when his grandma came to pick him up, he cried again."

"I see," Tom says.

"Emma asked him why he cries so much and that made him cry more. Why does he?"

"Cry so much?" Elizabeth asks.

Olivia nods.

"Sometimes people are sad," Elizabeth says. "And they just need time to be happy again."

"Will he be happy again?" Olivia asks.

"I'm sure he will," Tom says. "But you can keep praying for that to happen."

Tom pulls the pink blanket up to Olivia's chin and kisses her on the forehead. Elizabeth tucks Olivia's teddy beside her and kisses her on each cheek.

"Sweet dreams, Princess," Elizabeth says. "Love you bunches and bunches."

* * *

Every night, Grandma and I had the same routine. Even when I got older, parts of it remained. Like the part where she hugged me and kissed me on the cheek and told me how much she loved me and how proud she was of me before she went to bed. No one has ever loved me as much as Grandma. I thought that Bryan did. I thought he was my Prince Charming, coming to take me away. But I was wrong. So wrong. But that's a moment for another day.

The best part of our nightly routine was Grandma reading me a book. Of course, we said prayers, too. But the book always came first

"Got the book you want to read?" Grandma asked me, then five.

I grabbed a book from the bookshelf Grandma had found at a yard sale. She sanded and painted it and made it look like new. I loved my pink bookshelf.

"Didn't we just read that book last night and the night before and the night before that?" Grandma asked.

I nodded and my pigtails laced with purple ribbons bounced.

"Well, OK then. Hop on up."

I snuggled next to Grandma on the patched sofa. She slipped one arm around me and started to read, her index finger sliding under the words as she went.

I loved the story of Cinderella. How she went to the ball and met the prince and had mice for friends. Oh, and a fairy godmother who made all of her dreams come true. In my mind, the fairy godmother looked like Grandma, whose basic wardrobe was tan khakis and some sort of button-down blouse she made, usually a floral print.

Grandma tucked me in bed and placed a glass of water, half full, on my nightstand. I always liked to have a drink nearby so if I woke up and was thirsty, it would be right there.

I folded my hands and Grandma folded hers and we prayed together.

"Wait," I said when we got to the "Amen" part.

"And God bless Rachel and Grandma. Oh, and can you make Matt happy and love me like he loved my mom?"

I heard Grandma gasp, and I opened my eyes to see her wiping her blotchy face on her pajama sleeve.

I prayed and prayed my whole life for Matt to be happy, but he never was. I wanted him to be happy more than I wanted him to love me. I gave up on him loving me when he stopped coming around after Grandma kicked him out of the house. I wasn't mad that Grandma kicked him out. He kept wrecking things and made Grandma cry all of the time. It wasn't long after Grandma kicked him out that we moved into a small apartment where the landlord mowed the yard and did other outside work. My bedroom wasn't as big as it was in the house, but it was right next to Grandma's instead of down the hall and I liked that.

CHAPTER 7

Olivia sets her pink and purple princess table with her ceramic floral china set. There's a setting for her and her best friend, Emma, and one for Olivia's doll, Sadie, and one for Emma's doll, Nellie.

"Is it time yet?" Olivia calls to her mother.

"Almost," Elizabeth says.

Each week, the five-year-olds have a play date and this week it's at Olivia's house. The doorbell rings and Olivia races to the front door. The girls hug and Emma and Olivia run to the playroom where they'll spend most of the afternoon. The room is packed with every toy a little girl could want – from a play kitchen to an immense dollhouse to a puppet theater complete with a red velvet curtain.

Elizabeth walks in with a plate filled with grapes, carrot sticks, and peanut butter and jelly sandwiches cut into quarters, diagonally. She places a quarter on each girl's plate.

"Don't forget Sadie and Nellie," Olivia says. "They're hungry."

Elizabeth puts a quarter on their plates, too, and sets the rest in the middle of the table.

The girls dig in Olivia's sparkly pink dress-up trunk for hats and boas to wear. Olivia wears her Cinderella gown and Emma chooses the Snow White dress. Olivia picks the tea-party hat with the pink chandelle feathers and matching boa and short-sleeve gloves. Emma picks the tea-party hat with the ruffle trim and matching boa and long-sleeve gloves. They pull out the pink and purple chairs with heart-shaped cushions and place their dolls across the table from one another. Then they pull out the other two chairs and sit.

"What's that, Sadie? You think this is good? Me, too," Olivia says.

"Nellie thinks it's good, too," Emma says.

The girls' giggles draw a curious Elizabeth, who peeks in the room and finds them changing their dolls' diapers.

"You have a real baby sister to change," Olivia says. "I wish I did."

"Maybe you could ask Santa for one?"

Ever since Emma got a baby sister, Olivia's been asking her parents for one. They've told her that she's special, picked just for them and that even if she never has a baby sister, or brother, she can always have friends over to play. Olivia doesn't quite understand the why behind it, but having Emma over always helps.

* * *

"You're my bestest friend," Rachel said, hugging me.

It was the first — and only — time Rachel was allowed to play at my house. We spread the blanket out on the living-room floor and pretended to have a picnic on the beach. The tan vinyl hassock was a sand dune and the sofa was our sailboat. We had so much fun pretending – until Matt came home.

It was in the middle of the afternoon and Grandma was in the kitchen baking chocolate-chip cookies.

Matt opened the door and stumbled in with a woman whose top was cut so low that I thought her double-Ds would pop out. He knocked over the black tole-painted TV tray inside the front door where Grandma kept her keys. Grandma heard the noise and rushed into the hallway.

"Matt," Grandma said. "It's the middle of the afternoon. Sarah has a friend over."

Matt took a couple of steps toward Grandma, almost knocking her over. "I have a friend over, too." His speech was slurred. "This here's Candy."

"Matt," Grandma said. "Not now."

"Get out of my way, old woman," he said, swatting her with the back of his arm.

He looked at me. "What are you lookin' at, kid?"

I swallowed hard and stepped in front of Rachel to protect her. "Go. Don't hit Grandma."

Rachel was holding onto the back of my shirt so tightly that I thought it was going to rip.

"Oh, Mattie," the woman said. "Let's just go to my place."

Matt looked at Grandma, then at me.

They stumbled out the same door they came in and Grandma ran to the kitchen to take the burning cookies out of the oven. The kitchen filled with smoke and the fire alarm made a shrill sound, the kind that no matter how well you cover your ears, you still hear it.

* * *

"Want to play grown-ups?" Olivia asks.

Emma nods.

"I'm a dancer. What do you want to be?"

"A teacher."

The girls divide the room, each taking a half for her "apartment".

Olivia pretends to call Emma. "Were the kids good today in school?"

"There was one little boy who was bad. He pulled a girl's hair."

"What did you do?" Olivia asks.

"Gave him a timeout."

"Want to come over for dinner?" Olivia asks.

"What are you having?"

"Macaroni and cheese."

"The SpongeBob-shaped ones?" Emma asks.

"Yes," Olivia says.

"Be right over."

Elizabeth stands outside the room and smiles. I think she loves listening to the girls play. I know these moments are some of my favorite to record. Olivia and Emma act out what they see in real life.

* * *

One night, I was playing with my Barbie dolls in my bedroom. I was around five. I didn't know that Grandma could hear me.

"What are you doing here?" Barbie asked. "You can barely stand."

I made Ken wobble. "Come to get me some money."

"But I gave you money yesterday," Barbie said.

"And I need more today, woman."

"You know better than to come here like this," Barbie said.

"Are you going to give me the money or am I going to take it?"

Grandma walked in. Her hands shook. "No, no, no. That's not how we play."

She sat on the floor and picked up the Ken doll.

"Would you like to go out for dinner?" Grandma said in her best male voice.

"Ken doesn't like to go out to dinner. He likes to drink," I said. "He likes that bar around the corner."

Grandma shook her head. "He stopped drinking." Again, Grandma pretended to be Ken. "Would you like to go out to dinner?"

"That's too expensive. Why don't you pick up a roasted chicken at the grocery store and we can pretend that it came from a fancy restaurant?"

Grandma put the Ken doll down. "I can't play anymore," she said, and went to her room. I heard her crying.

CHAPTER 8

Olivia bites into an apple and her eyebrows jump to the top of her forehead. She pulls the apple away to look at it.

"Mom," she yells. "My tooth's in the apple."

Elizabeth sets down the basket of laundry. "So it's finally come out. That tooth has been dangling for days."

Olivia grabs some tissue and dabs the blood. She hands her mom the apple.

"Emma got a dollar for her tooth last week," Olivia says. "Wonder what the tooth fairy will bring me."

Elizabeth pulls the tiny tooth out of the apple. "Guess you'll have to put your tooth under your pillow tonight and see."

Olivia jumps up and down. "I have that special pillow Daddy bought me. It has a pocket for the tooth."

Elizabeth smiles. "I forgot about that. You'll have to show Daddy when he gets home."

* * *

By the time I lost my first tooth, Matt wasn't living with us anymore. Despite Grandma's efforts to get him help, he sank deeper and deeper into a drunken abyss.

Sometimes, I'd catch Grandma looking through old photos of Matt when he was a baby. She even showed me a lock of hair from his first haircut and a baby-food jar filled with his baby teeth. Grandma did the same for me. She kept a curl from my first haircut in a plastic baggie and she covered a baby-food jar with pink construction paper and wrote "Sarah's teeth" with a black marker on the side. I lost my first tooth at school.

"Look, Rachel," I said, pinching one of my bottom teeth with my thumb and index finger and wiggling it. "Grandma said it will come out soon."

"Want me to pull it?" Rachel asked. "My dad pulled mine and got it out."

I shook my head. I wasn't brave enough.

"It doesn't hurt," Rachel said. "I'll do it quick. Promise."

For a second or two, I considered Rachel's offer but the bell rang and we had to go back to our classroom. Recess was over.

I kind of forgot about my loose tooth until I took a bite of my peanut butter and jelly sandwich at lunch and something crunched in my mouth. I spit out the chewed blob of sandwich and found my tooth inside it.

"You did it." Rachel clapped.

Rachel was always my biggest cheerleader. No matter how bad something was, she'd always find something good in it.

* * *

Tom opens the car door for Olivia and bows as she slips into the back seat. It's daddy-daughter date night and they're headed to dinner and the ballet.

"When I grow up I want to be a ballerina," Olivia says.

"You'd make a beautiful ballerina. It takes a lot of practice, though."

"Miss Dawn says that we should practice every day, and I do."

Tom nods.

"Emma does karate. Why does she do that and not ballet?"

Tom smiles. "Because it's what she likes. Just like you like chocolate cake and Mommy likes vanilla. It's good when people like different things. If everyone liked the same thing, the world wouldn't be as interesting."

"But what if someone likes chocolate and vanilla?"

"That's OK, too. But sometimes you can only have one and you need to decide which one it will be."

"Why can't I have both?"

"We don't always get what we want, Libby. You're little and most of the things you have to decide are little like you. But when you get to be a big girl, the decisions will be harder to make. Sometimes you can have chocolate, sometimes you can have vanilla and sometimes, if you're lucky, you can have both."

I can see the wheels turning inside Olivia's head. She doesn't entirely understand, but I know that with age comes wisdom. I pray that the little girl I am keeping moments for will always get whatever flavor cake she wants.

* * *

I looked at the pink sign with green lettering on the school door. "Daddy-Daughter Dance."

"Are you going?" Tracey Carmichael asked.

Tracey was in my first-grade class.

I shook my head.

"Why not? It'll be fun."

"I don't have a dad."

Tyler Butler overheard me and walked over. "You do too have a dad. I've seen him. He rides a motorcycle and has tattoos on his arms and a red bandana on his head. My mom said he's a biker."

"He's not my dad."

"Then who is he?"

"His name's Matt."

I walked away from Tracey and Tyler. I didn't want to talk to them anymore. When I got home, Grandma asked me what was wrong. She said she could tell I was upset about something because I was extra quiet and I didn't want my usual afterschool snack of Oreos and apple juice.

A tear slipped from my eye, followed by another. Within seconds, it became a deluge. It was as if the tears had been holed up all day just waiting for the right moment to bust loose. "There's a dance for daddies and daughters and I don't have a daddy and everyone else does."

Grandma bent down and wrapped her saggy arms around me and kissed me on the forehead. "I'm sorry, Sarah. I wish things were different. But we don't always get the things that we want."

"Like the time I wanted chocolate-chip ice cream and there was only that yucky kind?"

"Exactly," Grandma said. "Sometimes yucky's all there is and you have to make the best of it."

"Like you putting chocolate syrup on it?"

Grandma nodded. "It made it taste better, didn't it?"

I smiled. "Yeah. It tasted better."

CHAPTER 9

"There she is!" Olivia yells.

Olivia, six, is dressed in her blue Cinderella gown with tulle petticoat. A bejeweled heart-shaped cameo accents the bodice.

She runs toward Cinderella Castle at Disney World and her beaded tiara with glitter organza ribbon flies off. Elizabeth picks up the tiara and places it back on Olivia's head.

Olivia gets in line behind two girls.

Olivia loves Disney World. Her parents take her every year. She loves seeing the princesses and getting their autographs. Elizabeth always makes her a keepsake album that includes all their favorite photos. Several albums line the bottom shelf of the bookcase in Olivia's room. One of Olivia's prized possessions is a pink lanyard covered with collectible Disney pins. She has dozens of them.

Cinderella is her favorite character. She always eats breakfast and dinner with Cinderella in Cinderella's castle. And she usually stops by the Crystal Palace at the end of Main Street for breakfast with Pooh and his friends and at Chef Mickey's at the Contemporary Resort for dinner with Mickey, Minnie and their friends. It's always a whirlwind week full of laughter and love and happiness. Wonderful moments to record.

* * *

I've never been to Disney World. I always wanted to go. I remember when I was in first grade and Tracey Carmichael came back from a trip to Disney World with a carriage-load of souvenirs. She brought them in for show and tell, a new thing each week. There were Minnie Mouse ears, a Cinderella dress and matching purse, a Snow White umbrella, jewelry and T-shirts and pens and pencils and markers. Oh, and a mug for the teacher and lollipops for everyone in the class. Everyone liked Tracey. And they liked her more when she gave them treats.

I remember asking Grandma if we could go to Disney and see Cinderella as Tracey did.

"And she had breakfast in Cinderella's castle," I said. "And there were fireworks and Tinkerbell flew down from the sky."

"She did?" Grandma said.

I nodded like Tracey's Mickey bobble head that she let everyone hold — everyone except me. She said that I was too clumsy, recalling the time I tripped over the carpet while carrying the classroom goldfish and dropped it on the floor. The fish died.

"Yeah, and Tracey said she got real pixie dust."

For the next several months, I bugged Grandma about going to Disney World. Tracey Carmichael wasn't the only one who went that year. Alex and Michael Deamer went and Katelyn White got to go, too.

Then one winter day Grandma said she had a surprise. We were going to see Mickey and Minnie and Pluto and Goofy and the rest of the Disney gang. But, she quickly added, we weren't going to Disney World.

I had seen Grandma put change in the empty red coffee container she kept in the cabinet near the sink. She explained that she had been saving money for a year to take me to see the Disney on Ice show coming to the area.

"I know it's not Disney World," Grandma said. "But you'll get to see the characters and you might even get their autographs."

I was so excited I could barely sleep that night. I kept checking the small glass container of pixie dust Grandma had given me when she told me about the show. I sat it on my nightstand when I went to bed. Looking back, it was probably a mixture of very fine blue and silver glitter. But to me, at that age, it was the real deal.

Just like Tinkerbell, Grandma had spread her magic dust and I was flying higher than I ever thought possible. Not even Tracey Carmichael could bring me down.

* * *

Tom watches Olivia get off the bus in front of their house. They live in a gated community with manicured lawns and colorful gardens; many have waterfalls and gazebos. Olivia skips toward Tom, her blonde pigtails bouncing and her pink princess backpack swinging from side to side.

Tom opens his arms and Olivia runs into them.

"I got a surprise for you," Tom says.

A smile erupts on Olivia's face, dusted with light freckles.

"Come with me."

Tom takes Olivia's hand and leads her to the patio behind the house where Elizabeth stands with a video recorder.

Olivia's eyes pop and she jumps up and down when she sees the pink sparkly bike with "Princess" printed on the crossbar. "Is it mine?"

"All yours," Tom says.

Olivia drops her backpack and climbs onto the seat and starts to pedal.

"Wait," Tom yells. "You never ever get on a bike without this."

He holds up a pink sparkly helmet and puts it on Olivia, adjusting the straps to make sure it fits tightly.

"Promise me you'll always wear a helmet," Tom says. "I just had a patient the other day who was hurt because he didn't wear a helmet."

Olivia knows from the tone of her daddy's voice that he is serious and means what he says. She doesn't often hear that tone, but when she does she knows she must pay attention.

"I promise," says Olivia, pedaling in a circle around the patio.

"Emma rides without wheels," Olivia says.

"We'll take the training wheels off when you think you're ready to ride without them," Tom explains.

Olivia follows Tom to the front of the house and he walks while she rides on the sidewalk down to the stop sign and back. After a few times down and back, Olivia gets brave and wants to go around the block. So, Tom takes her around the block, breaking a sweat as he runs to keep up with her.

* * *

I'll never forget my first bike. Someone had put it out for trash pickup and Grandma and I saw it on our way home from the grocery outlet.

Grandma pulled over to the curb next to the Hulk bike.

"What do you think, Sarah? Some new paint and a new seat and we'll have this bike looking as good as that bike you saw in the store."

"Are we allowed?"

"Sure we can take it," Grandma said. "These folks don't care. They want to get rid of it. Doesn't matter to them how that happens, whether it's the garbage men or us."

Grandma popped the trunk on the old Chevy and lifted the bike. I saw a woman watching from the window as Grandma eased the bike into the trunk then slammed it shut.

By the end of the week, Grandma had that bike looking better than any store-bought one. She painted it pink and added a pink and silver sparkly seat, a water-bottle holder and a bell. She even found a pink plastic basket with flowers to put on the front so I could haul stuff.

"Oh, Grandma," I said. "It's the best bike ever."

When I rode down the sidewalk, I felt like a peacock presenting his feathers. Kids playing in yards pointed as I rode by and I rang my bell. I was happy. I had a new bike. And it was better than anyone else's bike. I was certain of that.

CHAPTER 10

I watch Olivia sleep. She looks so peaceful in her pink canopy bed. She always sleeps with her right hand over her heart and the left one down across her belly button or off to the side. I was a Pledge-of-Allegiance-sleeper, too. That's what Grandma called it.

Olivia is restless tonight. She's having a bad dream. She's dreaming that she's riding her bicycle and a stranger approaches her in a van. She tries to ride away from him but no matter how hard she pedals, the bike doesn't move. I feel her anxiety and try to will her out of the dream. Sometimes, if I think happy thoughts and direct them toward her, I'm able to disrupt the nightmare. But tonight is a particularly bad one. She and her dad role-played different "bad person scenarios" earlier in the evening and this was one of them. Olivia screams and within seconds Elizabeth and Tom fly into her bedroom.

Tom flips on the light switch. Elizabeth leaps on the bed and wakes Olivia. "It's just a dream, sweetie. Just a dream."

Elizabeth holds Olivia in her arms and rocks her gently back and forth. Tom rubs her back.

"Shh. It's OK. Daddy and I are here."

"That's right, pumpkin. It's just a dream," Tom says.

They finally get Olivia calmed down and tucked in once more. I continue to record the moments – never stopping, never sleeping.

* * *

I remember when I was about Olivia's age, eight, I had this particularly bad dream. I thought Matt was going to take me away from Grandma and make me live with him. It was after Grandma kicked him out of the house. Occasionally, she would invite him to dinner and hope that he wasn't drunk. She never stopped reaching out, even though Matt pummeled her outstretched hands time and time again.

This one Sunday, she made her pot roast, which Matt loved, and his favorite dessert, chocolate cake with peanut butter icing. We rushed home from church so Grandma could make her homemade blueberry biscuits. He loved those, too.

Matt was late. Really late. In fact, he was so late that Grandma and I ate dinner and cleaned up. When he did show up, it was late afternoon.

I was playing with my Barbie dolls in my bedroom. Grandma had made me a Barbie house out of a bunch of old cardboard boxes she fastened together. It wasn't as fancy as the Barbie penthouse complete with an elevator that Tracey Carmichael had, but I liked it better because Grandma had made it. She even made Barbie clothes out of the same material she used to make my clothes so we could match.

I heard Matt first. It sounded as if someone fell against the apartment door.

"Grandma," I yelled. "Did you hear that?"

I found Grandma snoring on her favorite chair with the Sunday paper on her lap. I shook her arm to wake her.

"Someone's at the door."

Grandma put the paper on the coffee table. By the time she reached the door, Matt was inside, swaying and trying to remain on his feet.

"Matt," Grandma said. "I told you never to come here like this."

Matt looked at me, clutching my Barbie to my heart. "What ya lookin' at, kid?"

I looked down at the floor.

His speech was slurred. "Maybe you should come live with me?"

"Sarah," Grandma said. "Go to your room. I'll take care of this. It's not good to see your dad like this."

"He's not my dad," I yelled, and ran to my room, slamming my door and locking it. I could hear Grandma's muffled voice. It sounded as if she was in the kitchen. Probably making Matt coffee. That was usually what she did. Made him coffee and got him sober enough to ride his Harley home.

Matt left a couple of hours later. I came out of my bedroom and heard Grandma crying. I found her in the kitchen doing the dishes.

I hugged her waist and she bent over to brush the curls away from my face.

"I love you, Grandma," I said.

"I love you, too, Sarah. I wish you had a better dad."

"I don't want a dad. I want you."

"And you'll always have me, Sarah."

"And you won't let anyone take me?"

"Never."

That night, I dreamt that Matt kidnapped me while Grandma slept. I don't think I've ever screamed louder.

Grandma let me sleep with her. In fact, it was weeks before I slept in my bed. It was the worst nightmare ever and I kept having it over and over until Matt died. I didn't have it anymore after that.

* * *

Olivia sits on the couch next to her dad. Tom puts his arm around her, pulls her in close and kisses the top of her head.

"Do you like helping people, Daddy?" Olivia asks.

"Yep."

"Then why are you sad?"

"Today was a tough day."

"Why?"

"You know how when you fall and hurt yourself?"

"Like the time I fell out of Emma's tree house and broke my arm?"

"Yeah, like that. A doctor fixed your broken arm, right?"

Olivia nods.

"But doctors can't fix everything. Sometimes a person can't be fixed. They're too broken."

"Like my ball that got run over by the lawn mower?"

"Yeah. Like your ball. Sometimes there's just too much damage and you can't make something whole again."

I wondered why Tom was so sad. It wasn't like him to be this sad. In fact, I'm not sure I've ever seen him this upset about something that happened at work. He seemed to be hugging Olivia more than usual and I suspected that a child was involved.

"I want to be a doctor just like you," Olivia says.

"But I thought you wanted to be a ballerina."

"I want to be a ballerina and a doctor. And a teacher. Like Miss Bogart."

Tom smiles.

Olivia hops off the couch and returns with her white doctor's kit she got from Santa. She takes out all of the instruments and places them on the couch beside her dad.

"First, I'm going to listen to your heart."

She puts the electronic stethoscope that plays a heartbeat in her ears and listens to her daddy's heart.

"You got a little cough. You need a shot."

She grabs the squeaky syringe and gives him a shot in his left arm. She places the pretend bandage on his arm where she gave the shot and feels his forehead.

"You feel hot."

She picks up the thermometer with four temperature readings, holds it up to his mouth and selects the highest temperature. "You are hot."

Then she wraps the blood-pressure cuff around his arm and squeezes the pump, which makes the dial on the gauge spin. She wraps up her examination by checking his reflexes with the play hammer and his ears and throat with the light scope.

"You need to rest. Doctor's orders."

Later that night, after Olivia has fallen asleep beside him on the couch, Tom tells Elizabeth what happened in the ER that day.

"God, Liz, it was awful," he says. "There were so many bruises on that girl's tiny body that I couldn't find a patch of white anywhere."

Elizabeth dabs her eyes with tissues. The toddler had been bludgeoned to death by her mother's boyfriend. He had whipped her repeatedly with a video-game controller.

"And just because she had a dirty diaper," Tom says. "She was two, Liz. Two. And she never had a chance."

Tom tells Elizabeth that the neighbors heard the toddler screaming for her mother. The mother was in the next room stuffing her face with potato chips and watching the soaps. The screaming got so bad that the neighbors called the cops. But it was too late.

I understood now the depth of Tom's sadness and anger.

"God, after I pronounced her dead, I went to my car and cried, Liz. I've never done that before. But I felt so helpless. How can a human being do something like that?"

"He wasn't human," Elizabeth says. "He was an animal."

Tom leans against her and Elizabeth wraps her arms around him and kisses the top of his head. "I wish I could take away your pain," she says.

Tom sees Olivia's white doctor kit on the floor, and he smiles.

* * *

I used to love to pretend that I was a doctor. I remember the day we found my doctor's kit at the Goodwill store. It was brand new. Never been opened. Wasn't often I found a toy that had never been opened at the Goodwill store, but that was my lucky day. And I was even luckier because Grandma bought it, after she got the clerk to take a dollar less than the ticket price.

I brought that toy kit home and played and played and played with it. Grandma would lie on the couch and I would do all of the things I just recorded Olivia doing

– checking her reflexes, temperature and heart; taking her blood pressure; and giving her a shot.

Grandma even put some of the cinnamon candies we used to decorate Christmas cookies in an old plastic prescription container for me to use as pretend pills.

"How am I doing, Doc?" Grandma asked.

"Pretty good. But you need to make more cookies. That would make you feel better."

Grandma laughed. "Are you sure, Doc?"

"Yes. Making cookies will make you feel better. And maybe some brownies."

Grandma made the best chocolate-chip cookies in the whole universe. She didn't buy the ones you break apart and bake like Rachel's mom. She made them from scratch. And her brownies were good, too. Rachel's mom bought brownies. They came individually wrapped.

"You rest while I check on my other patients."

I always placed my dolls and stuffed animals around the room and pretended to do hospital rounds, visiting each patient.

I walked over to my stuffed panda bear, Lucy. "How are you today, Lucy?"

Grandma always provided the voices for my patients. "It hurts when I swallow."

"Let me check your throat." I grabbed the light scope. "Open wide. Just what I thought. Strep throat. Here's a pill."

I pretended to give Lucy a pill and moved to my next patient, a doll named Suzy who broke her arm. After examining Suzy, I used the roll of toilet paper Grandma had given me to use as pretend bandages and wrapped Suzy's arm. After seeing my other patients, I returned to Grandma.

"Do you think I could go home tomorrow?" Grandma asked.

"Yes," I said. "Provided you take this pill and get a good night's rest."

I gave Grandma one of the cinnamon-candy pills and she rolled it in her mouth until it dissolved.

"I feel all better," she said.

And she closed her eyes and pretended to be asleep, even pretend snoring for more effect.

How I wished I could have cured Grandma with a cinnamon-candy pill when she got so sick that she couldn't get out of her chair. Funny that as a child I could fix everything and as an adult, very little.

CHAPTER 11

Olivia holds a keepsake handprint plaque she made out of clay for Mother's Day.

"Do you think Mommy will like it?"

"No," Tom says, picking Olivia up and twirling her around. "She'll love it."

Tom puts Olivia down. "But you know what the best present she's ever received is?"

Olivia's gappy smile widens. She's been told this over and over.

"You," Tom says, tickling her belly.

Olivia giggles. "Do you think the lady's tummy I grew in will get a plaque?"

Tom catches his breath. "I don't know."

Tom and Elizabeth have been very open with Olivia about her adoption, always explaining to her in an age-appropriate way where she came from. They've told her over and over that they are her forever family and will always love her. Still, Olivia sometimes wonders about her birth mother.

I, too, have wondered about Olivia's birth mom. What kind of person was she? How old was she? Where did she live?

"Let's wrap mommy's present and then we'll go for ice cream like I promised."

Elizabeth is working at the hospital this weekend and when it's just Tom and Olivia on a Saturday night, they always go for ice cream. Olivia's favorite is vanilla with rainbow sprinkles.

* * *

When I was in kindergarten, we made pictures with our handprints for Mother's Day.

Miss Becky gave each of us a piece of white construction paper and told us to place our hand in the poster paint on the plate in the middle of the table then press it on the paper. After we washed our hands, we were to print our name and the year in our "very best printing".

"But Sarah doesn't have a mom," Reid said, wiping his snotty nose on his shirt sleeve.

Reid always had a snotty nose. His shirt always looked as if it had snail tracks on it. I knew what snail tracks looked like because I'd seen them on our screen door at home.

Rachel put her hands on her hips and gave Reid her squinty I-going-to-punch-you-in-the-noggin look. "She has a grandma."

"That doesn't count. It's not the same."

Rachel raised her hand. "Miss Becky, can you tell Reid that Sarah can make a picture for her Grandma since she doesn't have a mom."

"That's right, Reid. Sarah's grandmother is her mom."

"But my grandma's not my mom. She's my mom's mom."

Reid always was a smarty pants. That's something that never changed. It only got worse the older he got. By the time we were in high school, I stopped being in his classes. He was always in classes with the super-smart kids. I wasn't so smart. Or maybe I just didn't try.

But Reid's comments did make me wonder about my mom, sort of like Olivia wonders about her mom. Grandma said my mom loved me, but I could never figure out why Matt, if he loved my mom so much, didn't love me.

I know she died when she had me, but Grandma always told me that my mom knew she was going to die. That she chose my life over hers. Grandma said Matt let anger eat away at him like a cancer. When Grandma got cancer, I saw just what she meant. The eating-away part, I mean.

* * *

"Daddy," says Olivia, sitting in a booth at the ice-cream shop. "That boy scares me."

She points to a red-haired boy about her age with big ears and a Band-Aid on his forehead sitting across from his dad.

Tom looks in the direction Olivia is pointing. "Why? He doesn't look scary to me."

"He has his dad's eyes."

"What?" Tom asks.

"The lady who gave him his ice cream said that he has his dad's eyes. And she pointed to that man across from him. And if he has his dad's eyes, then his dad doesn't have any eyes."

Tom laughs and tears pool in Olivia's green eyes. "Oh, princess," Tom says. "It's not what you think. That little boy didn't take his daddy's eyes. His daddy still has his eyes. The lady meant that his eyes *look* like his daddy's."

Olivia breathes a sigh of relief. "Do I have your eyes?"

Tom runs his fingers through his hair. This is the second tough question of the night and I wonder how he's going to answer. "No, you don't have my eyes. But we see the same thing with our eyes."

Olivia smiles. His answer satisfies her – for now.

* * *

I asked Grandma once if I had my mom's eyes. I knew I had her blonde curly hair. Grandma had told me that. But I wondered about her eyes. We were studying dominant and recessive genes in high school and our assignment was to see how our eye color compared to our parents'. My dad had brown eyes and Grandma told me that my mom had green eyes. I was glad I ended up with my mom's eye color. It was bad enough I had my dad's dimples. I hated those dimples. I didn't want to have anything of his. I had always planned to get my dimples fixed when I got older and could afford it. I had read in my teen magazine that you could get them fixed.

"But, Sarah," Grandma said the day I told her how much I hated my dimples. "When you smile your dimples are like exclamation points."

"It's a birth defect, Grandma," I said in my know-it-all-teen voice. "A defect just like Matt."

Grandma cried when I said that. I was mean and I shouldn't have been. But Matt was meaner and Grandma knew it. Even so, I think I broke her heart that day. She had dimples, too.

* * *

I look at Olivia. She has dimples, too, and I don't think they look like a defect. I think they look cute, just as Grandma thought mine looked cute.

Ice cream drips from Olivia's cone onto the red laminate tabletop.

"Lick around the edges," Tom says, placing a couple more napkins in front of Olivia.

Tom finishes his dish of raspberry ice cream. Steam snakes upward as the waitress refills his white coffee mug. He picks it up and takes a sip. "So what movie do you want to watch when we get home?"

"Snow White."

"Didn't we watch that the last time Mommy worked?" Olivia nods.

"And you want to watch it again?"

Olivia nods again, trying to lick her cone faster than it can melt. She has been on a Snow White kick lately.

"OK. We'll watch Snow White, but maybe the next time we can watch something different."

Olivia nods.

* * *

I know what it's like to love a movie. I loved Bambi. It wasn't one of Grandma's favorites. I noticed that she always left the room when Bambi's father told him that his mother couldn't be with him anymore.

"That's kind of like my mother," I told Grandma the first time we watched the movie. Rachel had all of the Disney movies and let me borrow them.

Grandma put her hand to her heart. "Come again, Sarah?"

"Bambi's mom died like my mom, but she saved him just like my mom saved me."

Grandma dabbed the corners of her eyes with one of her handmade cotton hankies. "Well, I suppose in a way it is," she said.

"Was it my fault, Grandma, that she died?"

"Oh, come here."

I jumped off the couch and bounced over to Grandma, who was sitting in her favorite rocker. She sat up straight, brushed the curls off my face, put her hands on my shoulders and looked me straight in the eyes. "Don't you ever, ever think that it was your fault. Your mother wanted you more than anything. When she got sick, instead of saving herself, she saved you. And just like Bambi, you're going to grow up and experience great things. Promise me that, Sarah."

"I promise."

I had forgotten about our Bambi discussion and my promise. In a matter of seconds I had broken my promise to Grandma, and a raging fire of guilt consumed me.

CHAPTER 12

Olivia and Emma approach a two-story brick house with its porch light on. Just as Olivia is about to ring the doorbell, a short woman with salt and pepper hair and pointy glasses opens the door.

"Trick or treat," the girls say.

"What do we have here?" the lady says.

"I'm a cat," Olivia says. "See?" And she turns in a circle to show her long black tail.

"And I'm a cheerleader," Emma says. She shakes her blue and white pom-poms.

"You're a very pretty cat," the lady says, "and you're a very pretty cheerleader." She puts a chocolate bar in each of their plastic Halloween bags.

Olivia's dad waits on the sidewalk as the eight-year-olds go from house to house. Olivia's neighborhood is the type of neighborhood I would have loved to have gone trick or treating in when I was her age. She gets full-size candy bars at nearly every house. One couple even fires up the grill and gives away hot dogs and orange drinks to kids and parents.

In the apartment complex where Grandma and I lived, most people gave out lollipops or Smarties. Chocolate was a real treat. And when you got it, it was the miniature candy bars, never the full-size ones.

Olivia and Emma skip up the sidewalk to the next house. As they approach the porch they see three older boys standing in front of a bench with a big black plastic cauldron filled with giant Reese's peanut butter cups. One boy is dressed as a pirate, one as a ninja and the other is wearing a scary mask that looks as if it got caught in a meat slicer. With its cuts and gashes and blood, it's the scariest mask Olivia and Emma have ever seen.

Olivia sees the sign taped to the candy bowl. It says: Take one, please.

"Look at all that candy," Scary Mask says. "We could take it all. They'd never know."

Olivia and Emma look at each other. Olivia swallows hard. "No, that's wrong."

Scary Mask turns around. "Says who?"

Olivia steps forward a little bit more and looks Scary Mask straight in the eye holes. "Says me."

"You're gonna let some girl tell you what to do?" Pirate Boy says.

Scary Mask doesn't say anything and Olivia hasn't stopped staring him down.

"Everything all right, Lib?" Tom calls from the sidewalk.

The boys look toward Tom and then back at Olivia and Emma.

"Just take one for now," Scary Mask says. "We can come back for the rest later."

The boys grab one giant peanut butter cup and race to the next house.

"I could never be as brave as you," Emma tells Olivia.

"Yes, you could," Olivia says. "Daddy says to stand up for what's right, even if that means you're standing alone. Taking all the candy wouldn't have been right."

* * *

Emma's right. Olivia is brave for an eight-year-old. It isn't the first moment I've captured where she's flexed her tiny muscles against a much bigger kid. There was the time an older girl butted in line at the golden carousel at the amusement park and Olivia made her go to the end of the line. And the time Kevin from gym class called Olivia's friend Elf Ears because he had big ears that stuck straight out. Olivia told Kevin that at least Ryan would grow into his ears but that he would be stuck with his big mouth forever. Kevin didn't like that too much, but no matter what comeback he had, Olivia always had a better one. Olivia was quick on her feet and always a champion for the underdog.

* * *

When I was Olivia's age, I was more like Emma, quiet and a bit reserved. Definitely a follower. I might have wanted to stand up for what I thought was right or to defend myself, but I never had the courage to actually do it. There was this kid, Jeremy the Jerk, who teased me about my webbed toes. The two toes beside my big toe on each foot were connected. I was born this way. Grandma used to tell me it made me special. I never bothered to have them separated, even though Grandma said that if I wanted to she'd save up to have it done. But Jeremy the Jerk, who noticed them one day at the apartment pool, called me Duckie every chance he got.

"What's wrong with your toes?" asked Jeremy, who was behind me in line for the diving board.

I curled my toes and turned my head. "Nothing."

"I saw them. They're stuck together. Like a duck's."

The boys behind him laughed, which egged Jeremy on and he turned up the teasing a notch.

"Quack! Quack! Quack!" he shouted, flapping his arms as if they were wings.

My face got pizza-oven hot and it wasn't from the scorching sun. Tears pooled in my eyes and I tried to be brave and hold them back but I couldn't. I decided that I didn't want to go off the diving board anymore. Instead, I found Grandma and stayed on my beach towel – legs crossed Indian-style so I could hide my feet – until she was ready to go home.

I became good at hiding things I didn't want other people to know. It's one of the reasons no one knew I was pregnant – not even Grandma. Course, by then she was so sick it took all of her energy to get through the day.

* * *

"Were those boys giving you trouble, Libby?" Tom asks the girls as they join him at the end of the block before going on to the next street.

"They were going to take all of the candy but Libby stopped them," Emma says.

"Did you know the boys?"

"The one sounded familiar, but he was hiding behind that scary mask so I'm not sure," Olivia says. "But if I hear his voice again, without the mask, I'll remember."

* * *

Matt was like Scary Mask. I was terrified of him and what he could do if he wanted. After he agreed to let Grandma adopt me, I wasn't as afraid.

"Matt, you smell like rotten garbage and look just as bad," Grandma said one night when Matt stopped by while on one of his binges.

"Give me some money, old woman, and don't worry about the smell."

"I'm not giving you another dime. I've given you enough."

I heard the yelling and scrambled out of bed and stood behind Grandma, clutching her robe.

Matt looks at me. "What about her? You gonna give her all your money?"

"I'll make a deal with you, Matt. You give me Sarah. Sign those papers I gave you a while back and I'll write you a check."

"How much?"

"As much as I can afford. Maybe a thousand."

"You really want her that bad?"

"Yes," Grandma said. "I think Sarah would be better with me."

He sliced the air with his hand. "You can have her."

He looked at me. "That what you want?"

I nodded. It was the only time he had asked me what I wanted.

Matt turned and staggered to the door. "I'll sign those damn papers as soon as I get home. A thousand sounds good."

CHAPTER 13

Olivia walks into her bedroom and tosses her ballet bag on her bed. I see Oscar is dead before she does. I know the blue betta fish sleeps a lot, but he's definitely not sleeping now. Olivia walks over to feed him.

"You sleep too much, Oscar," she says.

She taps her finger on the side of the glass fish bowl but Oscar doesn't respond. She picks up the bowl and jiggles it. Still, no movement.

"Mom," Olivia yells. "Something's wrong with Oscar."

Elizabeth walks in carrying a basket of laundry. "Maybe he's sleeping."

"He won't wake up when I tap the bowl, and he usually always wakes up when I tap."

Elizabeth sets the wash basket down and walks over and taps on the bowl, too. She picks up the bowl to get a closer look. "I'm sorry, Libby. But I think Oscar's dead."

Olivia's eyes turn glassy and her lips tremble as she tries to be a big girl and keep her eight-year-old self from crying. But she loses the battle and bursts into tears. "I killed him. It's my fault. I'm a bad fish mommy."

Elizabeth wraps her arms around the heaving Olivia. "It's not your fault Oscar died, Libby. Fish don't live forever."

"Maybe I didn't change his water enough or feed him enough."

"It wasn't either of those things. You couldn't have been a better fish mommy. Fish get old and die. Just like people. It's a part of the circle of life."

"Will you and Daddy die?"

Elizabeth nods. "But hopefully not for a very long time."

At eight, it's Olivia's first experience with death, and I know that the realization of not having her parents forever has hit her like an unexpected summer storm. She never saw the darkness that lurked behind that beautiful robin-egg sky. Just naturally took for granted that her parents would always be with her.

* * *

The first dead thing I ever saw was Matt. I had just turned thirteen.

I'll never forget the morning Grandma got the call. I was still in bed and she flew into my room as if the apartment were on fire.

"Sarah," Grandma said, shaking my shoulder. "You gotta get up. We gotta get to the hospital. Your dad's been in an accident."

Grandma rushed to her room to get dressed and I tumbled out of bed and threw on some sweats and a T-shirt.

By the time we got to the hospital, it was too late. Matt was dead. The police said he had been riding his motorcycle without a helmet and turned left in front of a truck. The trucker tried to swerve to miss Matt, but he couldn't swerve fast enough. Matt slammed into the truck so hard that his bike slid under it.

Grandma cried. I didn't shed one tear.

A nice lady at the hospital escorted Grandma and me to a quiet room at the end of a long hallway. It contained a blue vinyl sofa and a couple of matching chairs. She asked if Grandma needed anything or wanted her to stay until the doctor arrived, but Grandma told her to go but that she'd appreciate a box of tissues. The woman returned almost immediately and placed the tissues on the wooden coffee table.

I sat beside Grandma on the couch, resting my head on her shoulder. She wrapped her arm around me and pulled me close, kissing the top of my head.

"You OK?" Grandma asked.

"Yeah. Are you?"

"I just wish I could have helped your dad."

"You tried," I said.

"Maybe I should have tried harder."

She sniffed. "I found the Cheerio."

I sat up and looked at Grandma. "What are you talking about? What Cheerio?"

Grandma stared at the wall, as if she was trying to remember every detail of the story she wanted to share. "You were little. Just a baby, sitting in your high chair eating Cheerios one morning. Matt walked in and you said 'Da. Da. Da.' And you picked up a Cheerio and offered it to him. He didn't think I was watching. But I was. He took the Cheerio and put it in his pocket. After I kicked him out, I found the Cheerio in his nightstand drawer, along with a photo of your mother."

The door opened and the doctor walked in. She had brown hair tied back in a knot. She wore a white coat and a stethoscope circled her narrow neck. "I'm sorry. Your son's internal injuries were substantial."

"Anything worth saving for someone else?" Grandma asked.

The doctor nodded.

"Then make sure you take anything out that can help someone else. Maybe they'll appreciate them. Take care of them. God knows Matt never did."

Even through her black glasses, I saw the doctor's eyebrows jump. "Uh. OK. We can do that. Would you like to see him?"

Grandma looked at me. I shook my head no. Grandma looked at the doctor. "Can she wait here?"

"Sure," the doctor said. "Follow me."

Grandma left and I sank back into the vinyl couch. I felt a little guilty because I didn't cry and wasn't sad that Matt was dead. I figured that as far as he was concerned, the only good thing about me was that he got a thousand bucks to spend on cheap vodka. In the end, I was nothing more than one of his poker chips that he cashed in when he was hard up for cash for booze. But I did wonder about the Cheerio. He didn't seem like a Cheerio-keeping kind of guy.

It seemed like it took forever until Grandma came back. When she did, she didn't say much and I didn't ask anything. I figured that if and when Grandma wanted to talk about it she would.

The last time I saw Matt he was lying in a cold silver coffin wearing the white shirt and black pants Grandma bought at the Goodwill store the day after he died. He looked old. I wondered what parts of his body they took out of him and if those who had received the parts knew they came from a drunken bastard.

There were just the flowers that Grandma bought for on top of the casket. Grandma placed a wedding photo of Matt and my mom beside him in the casket. A few of Grandma's friends came, but that was it.

I kept thinking Matt would wake up. I didn't want him to wake up. I felt horrible thinking that, but it meant I didn't have to worry that he might change his mind and want me back. I didn't have one good memory of Matt. Not one. There was no life to celebrate and remember, only joy that the drunken bastard was gone for good.

* * *

"Can we bury him in the backyard?" Olivia asks Elizabeth.

"Sure. Let me see if I can find a box."

Elizabeth returns with a white jewelry box. "We can put him in here."

Elizabeth scoops out Oscar and places him on top of the cotton lining. Olivia's hand trembles as she puts on the lid.

"Will he go to Heaven?" asks Olivia, sniffling.

Elizabeth nods. "Of course he will. So don't be sad. He's in heaven having a great time with all of his other fish friends."

"And people, too, right?"

"And people, too."

* * *

I thought that when Matt died, he probably went straight to Hell and that my mom was probably sad that he wasn't good enough to make it into Heaven.

We buried Matt beside my mom in the old, overgrown Lutheran cemetery on the edge of town. I had come to this cemetery many times with Grandma to place flowers on my mom's grave. There was no stone on her grave until a few years ago. Grandma had an envelope that she saved money in over the years to pay for a grave marker. It wasn't anything fancy. A few flowers etched in a small gray granite marker, but it was at least something.

My mom didn't have any life insurance, so Grandma worked out a deal with the undertaker. There was a little insurance on Matt, enough to pay for the casket and some other things. But Grandma skipped the obituary in the paper. She thought it was one cost she could eliminate. Maybe she figured the news story about the crash was enough to tell people he was dead. And, besides, most of the obituaries were filled with flowery stuff about how great the person was. There wasn't anything even remotely great about Matt.

* * *

Olivia helps Elizabeth dig a hole beside the towering snowball bush in the corner of the yard. The shrub, with its big white snowball-like flower clusters, has always been Olivia's favorite plant.

Olivia puts the box into the hole and scoops the dirt on top of it. She pats the ground. "Now we need a grave marker. Can I use one of the extra landscaping stones Daddy has in the garage?"

"Sure," Elizabeth says. "I'll get the stone and you get a marker."

Elizabeth returns with a flat stone and places it on top of the fresh grave. "You can do the rest."

Olivia takes the lid off of her black permanent marker and writes on the stone: Oscar the fish.

* * *

There was room left on my mom's marker for Matt's name. I think Grandma had planned it like that. Smart move on her part because it saved money. Didn't have to squirrel away money for another ten years.

"How many spots are there here?" I asked Grandma when we went to the cemetery to see the tombstone after Matt's name had been added.

"Your grandpa bought a lot for six. So there's plenty of room here for me when I go."

"That better not be for a really long time," I said.

"I don't plan on it, Sarah. But life has a way of dealing us stuff we don't plan on."

"But who would take care of me?"

I really didn't want to know the answer to that and I don't think Grandma really wanted to answer the question. Truth was I'd end up in foster care like my mom. We had no family, no relatives, no one who would take me in. If something happened to Grandma, I might as well die myself.

CHAPTER 14

Olivia sits Indian style on the living-room floor in front of the eight-foot Fraser fir decorated with white lilies and crystal spheres. Cousins, some older and others younger, surround her. They laugh, unable to sit still. One male cousin rubs his hands and another bites her fingernails.

Tom whistles to quiet the crowded room. "I want to thank everyone for celebrating Christmas with us once again. Liz, Libby and I always look forward to what's become a holiday tradition."

Tom looks at Elizabeth. "How long have we been doing this now?"

"Since Libby's first Christmas and she's nine," Elizabeth answers.

All eyes find Olivia and her face pops like a firework – green eyes sparkling, smile bursting, face as red as the roses her dad gave her mom that morning.

"That's right. Since Libby's first Christmas. We've welcomed a couple babies into the family since then and some of our loved ones are no longer with us and we should remember them tonight."

Heads nod and whispers of "yes" fill the great room.

"Please, eat up and have fun."

Sleigh bells ring. The kids stand and jump up and down. They know that Santa has arrived.

Santa, aka Uncle Ned, walks into the room carrying a huge red sack filled with gifts. He takes one gift out of the bag and calls the name on the tag. It's for Olivia's cousin, Samantha. Three-year-old Samantha skips to Santa and takes the gift.

"Ho! Ho! Ho!" Santa says. "Remember, don't open your gift until everyone has one. I'll go fast, I promise."

Santa calls one name after another and the kids get their gifts and then sit down, legs crossed and the gift on the floor in front of them. Olivia's fingers are crossed. I know that she's hoping for a dog. She's asked over and over for one, promising to take care of it all on her own.

Olivia looks around the room. Everyone has a gift but her. She wonders if Santa forgot her this year.

"Ho! Ho! Ho!" Santa says. "I have one gift that wouldn't fit in my Santa sack."

Tom hands him a big box with a red bow on top.

Santa reads the tag. "This one's for Olivia."

Santa sets the white box in front of Olivia.

"Why don't we let Olivia open hers first?" Santa says.

The kids gather around Olivia. There's a "yelp" from inside the box. Olivia tears off the bow, pushes back the flaps and reaches in.

"It's a puppy! It's a puppy! I got a puppy."

She picks up the five-pound Cairn terrier with a pink collar accented with rhinestones. Her dark eyes and black nose take up most of her puppy face. Her little ears fold down in perfect triangles.

Olivia lifts the puppy to her face and rubs her cheek against the puppy's quivering body. "It's OK, Daisy. You're with me now."

"Can I hold her?"

"I want to hold her."

"I get her next."

"Now, kids," Santa says. "Let's let Olivia hold her for a while. Then maybe later you can hold her."

"Uh-oh!" Olivia says.

"What's wrong?" Tom asks.

"I think Daisy just peed on me."

Olivia holds out Daisy and there's a big wet spot on the front of her green velvet dress. Everyone laughs.

"I'm sure it won't be the last time she pees on you," Tom says. "Come with me, Lib, and we'll take her out while the others open their gifts."

Tom and Olivia take Daisy out and the room erupts in total chaos – kids scream, paper flies every which way and all the adults can do is pray that nothing gets broken and nobody gets hurt.

I love Christmas at Olivia's house. Each year on Christmas Eve, both sides of the family gather for the biggest party of the year. The house is wrapped in laughter and love.

Long banquet tables are filled with food. There's steamed shrimp, pecan-crusted chicken tenders, caramelized onion brie en croute, bacon-wrapped sirloin gorgonzola skewers, artichoke and spinach filo tartlets, edamame dumplings and much more.

The desserts are just as amazing and include everything from red velvet cupcakes to eggnog cheesecake with gingersnap crust and pomegranate glaze. And cookies, lots of cookies, for the kids.

I imagine how everything would taste. Olivia especially likes the pecan-crusted chicken tenders and her favorite cookie is sand tarts. It's just about the only item on the tables that hasn't been prepared by a caterer. Grandma Cindy and Olivia always spend a day making sand tarts. Grandma Cindy takes Olivia shopping for special Christmas tins that Olivia puts cookies in to give to her teachers.

The night of the party, kids run from room to room, playing with the toys Santa has brought. The adults are always in good moods. They eat and drink and become kids again. Then the next day, Olivia always finds a mountain of gifts by the tree. While Santa stopped by in person the night before, he always surprises Olivia in the morning with even more things.

I have never seen so many gifts for one person in my life. And they are always wrapped in ballerina-themed paper. No other gifts in the house are wrapped in this paper, a sure sign, according to Tom, that Santa brought them.

Olivia always opens the cerise and pink crochet Christmas stocking Grandma Cindy made her last.It's always filled with little surprises and usually, at the toe of the stocking, is something extra special, like a birthstone ring.

* * *

My Christmases were nothing like Olivia's. Most of my gifts came from the dollar store and the others through the Salvation Army's Angel Tree program. Each year, Grandma filled out a registration sheet with the items I needed. The charity wrote the items people submitted on paper angels and hung them on trees at area businesses. People would pick an angel off a tree and buy the items listed. There was one angel for each child.

I always got pajamas and underwear, things that Grandma didn't feel right buying used at the Goodwill store. But there was usually something fun, like a toy, to go with it. And our church always gave us a box of food and a turkey so we always had a nice Christmas dinner.

When I got too old for the Angel Tree, Grandma said that I would get only three gifts. One for each of the wise men.

"I wish I could give you more," Grandma said. "But I got too many bills."

"Gram. Who cares about gifts anyway? You don't have to buy me anything. I don't buy you anything."

"You're my gift, Sarah," Grandma said. "And I thank the good Lord for you every day."

"But that's not the same as getting something," I said. "Like a new toaster. Only the one side works on the one we have and that'll probably go soon. And I know how much you love your toast in the morning."

"I'll look at the Goodwill store the next time I stop. I'll get me a toaster soon enough. If they don't have one, I'll tell Phyllis, the clerk who goes through the donations, to keep her eye out in case one comes in. She'll put it back for me. She's done that a time or two before when I needed something special."

I never had any money to buy Grandma gifts so I made things to give her. When I was little, I dug a coffee can out of the trash and covered it with a piece of white construction paper that I had decorated with blue and red stars. Then I wrapped it using paper Grandma had saved from presents we had received. In our house, Grandma always recycled, from empty bread bags to plastic grocery bags. She found a use for everything.

"It's a drum," I told Grandma when she unwrapped it that Christmas.

"Just what I always wanted," Grandma said. "A drum to play. And I love the red and blue stars."

Grandma sat the drum on her dresser and every now and then she would parade around the house tapping on the plastic lid. She acted as if that drum was the best gift she had ever received. When she died, I put the drum in her casket, just in case she wanted to play it in Heaven.

* * *

Olivia comes in from outside with Daisy and the puppy snuggles in her arms. She takes Daisy to her room, away from the other kids. She doesn't want to share Daisy just yet. She sits on her bed.

"You're the best present ever," Olivia tells Daisy. "I will always take care of you just like Mommy and Daddy take care of me."

Elizabeth is listening outside Olivia's room. She smiles and walks in.

"Ready to join everyone else?"

"Do I have to share Daisy?"

"Well, it would be nice to let the other kids hold her. Just for a little."

Olivia's shoulders drop and she sighs. "OK. If I have to."

* * *

I begged Grandma for a puppy but the closest I ever got was a toy one that, with the help of a battery pack, walked, sat, flipped over and barked. We found it at a yard sale and the lady put batteries in it to show us it still worked.

"You know we can't have any pets in the apartment," Grandma said.

"Why do we have to live in a stupid apartment anyway?" I shot back.

"Because it's what I can afford."

"Well, I'm tired of being poor. Everyone else has a puppy but me."

"Not everyone," Grandma said.

"Almost everyone. Rachel does. And some kids at school got them for Christmas."

"Sorry," Grandma said. "Even if we could have one in the apartment, I'd never have the money to spend on keeping a dog. They cost money. Just like humans, they got to go to the doctor's when they get sick and for checkups and shots. Plus, you got to buy them food. Just too much money."

I marched to my bedroom and slammed my door. I was a brat and Grandma deserved better.

* * *

The kids gather around Olivia and Daisy, and Olivia gives each one a turn holding the puppy. Grandma Cindy is talking to Elizabeth. They are standing nearby so I can hear them.

"One of my Angel gifts didn't have one toy listed," Grandma Cindy says. "It was all essential stuff, like underwear and socks and mittens. But I just had to add a toy or two. Every kid should have at least one toy to open Christmas morning."

"Olivia loved going shopping for her Angel gifts," Elizabeth says. "Tom brought home two from work. One was a little boy, eight, and the other a little girl, six."

I smiled. It was fun to watch Olivia pick out gifts for other children, and I couldn't help remember that I had been on the receiving end of such generosity growing up. When I got older, Grandma insisted that we give back. So, we participated in the Salvation Army's Red Kettle Christmas Campaign. Grandma would sit next to the tripod holding the red kettle and I would ring the bell, hoping people would make a donation. My cheeks always hurt from smiling so much. People always seemed more willing to give around Christmas, I thought. I never understood why that feeling couldn't last the whole year.

CHAPTER 15

Olivia sees Elizabeth and Tom pull into the driveway. They are returning from a parent-teacher conference with Olivia's fourth-grade teacher, Mrs. Beshore.

It's the first time I notice how Olivia's left eye and thumb twitch when she's nervous or stressed.

Olivia greets them at the door. "Did she say anything bad?"

She steps to the side so her parents can walk into the house.

"She said you're an excellent student but there is one thing you need to work on," Tom says.

Olivia follows her parents into the living room where Grandma Cindy is knitting Olivia another scarf. Olivia sits on the chair and her mom and dad sit on the sofa facing her.

Elizabeth starts. "You're way ahead in reading and writing and where you're supposed to be in math. But, you talk too much."

Olivia knew she was going to get in trouble for her talking. Just that day, Mrs. Beshore made her spend her recess writing, "I will not talk in class."

"But I have so much talking to do and there's never enough time to do it."

"Listen, Libby," Tom says. "We're glad that you're outgoing and sociable and everyone's friend. But when the teacher is teaching, you can't be talking. It's disrespectful and rude. And it needs to stop."

Olivia looks down. "OK, I'll try."

Grandma Cindy looks up from her knitting needles. "Sounds like someone else I know." Grandma Cindy smiles at Elizabeth. "Go on. Tell her about it."

"Mom."

"No Mom me. You were a talker, too, and just like Libby you had to learn how to zip up during class."

Olivia looks at her mom. "So you liked talking, too?"

"Did she ever," Grandma Cindy says. "She was always spending recesses inside or staying after school. Like mother, like daughter."

"OK, yes, I did like to talk," Elizabeth says. "But that doesn't mean you're off the hook. Like your dad said, you can't talk when you're not supposed to. Not only will it impede your learning, because if you're talking you're not listening, but that of others."

"What's impede mean?" Olivia asks.

"Hamper. Hinder. Hurt. Not only will it hurt your learning but it will hurt the other boys and girls because you talking gets in the way of their listening."

Olivia chews her lower lip. "OK. I'll try harder."

"That's all we're asking for, Libby. That you work on it," Tom says. "We don't expect you to become a silent wallflower because that's just not who you are, but we do expect you to be respectful."

* * *

To me, Olivia was a forget-me-not with its five blue lobes and a bright yellow center. After you met her, you never forgot her. She had a contagious energy that endeared her to others and made them want to be her friend.

I was a wallflower. Unlike Olivia, I never got in trouble for talking too much. In fact, I didn't talk enough. My teachers thought something was wrong with me. They put me through a bunch of testing. Turned out I was smart, just quiet. Besides Rachel, I didn't have any friends.

I envied girls like Olivia who were so happy and carefree and outgoing. Just the other day I watched Olivia walk into the ballet studio and all of the girls rushed toward her. It was as if she were the queen bee and they were the worker bees. They couldn't help but be attracted by her sunshiny optimism. Grandma told me once that I wear a frown like a piece of favorite clothing. She was right. I wish she had been wrong, but she was always right.

* * *

Elizabeth loads Olivia's costumes into the back seat of their tan Mercedes Benz. Tonight is Olivia's dance recital, and she's performing in numerous numbers – jazz, tap, ballet, modern.

Olivia's smile takes up most of her heart-shaped face. With her hair pulled back in a tight bun and eye shadow and mascara on, she looks older than nine.

I've watched Olivia dance since she was three, and I've never seen her happier than when she's on stage. And, as her moment keeper, I feel the greatest joy at these moments. I'm filled with intense warmth, not the fleeting kind that comes and goes, but a warmth that hangs on like a summer haze.

Olivia and the stage are like a lock and key – they fit perfectly. When opened, everything else falls away except for Olivia, a whirl of movement so beautiful that it grabs your breath before you know it's been taken. I have never seen someone dance as naturally as she dances. It's no wonder that her parents have decided to enroll her in the most prestigious dance academy in the state. Even if it does require them to travel more. Olivia is that good, and they know it. All she wants to do is dance. That is her dream.

* * *

I'll never forget the time Rachel talked me into participating in the talent show. We were in fifth grade. It was the one and only time I was on a stage. I hated being in the spotlight. I was more comfortable hiding in the dark wings, out of view.

"Rachel, you're next," Grandma said.

I stepped to the side so Grandma could measure Rachel.

"You girls are about the same size," said Grandma, rolling up her yellow tape measure. "Are you sure you like the material?"

Rachel and I nodded. Grandma was making us matching outfits for a skit/dance number that we, well, mostly Rachel, had choreographed. She was making us red pants with elastic waistbands and short-sleeve white tops with red polka dots that tied in the front. She found the material on the clearance rack and picked it up for pennies.

"Well, OK, then. I should have your outfits done by the end of the week."

Rachel and I hugged Grandma. By the night of the talent show, we had practiced our number so many times that even Rachel's dog left the room when he saw us moving the furniture so we had room to dance. Normally, that shaggy mutt wouldn't leave Rachel's side.

That's why I could never figure out what happened the night of the show. Maybe it was because Grandma had a severe case of bronchitis and couldn't come. Maybe I was nervous because we followed Tracey Carmichael, who wore the most beautiful ballet costume I had ever seen. It was pink with sequins and pearls on the bodice and a tutu with four layers of heavily gathered tulle.

I'm not sure what it was, but I froze. I couldn't move. So Rachel did what she always did. She covered for me. She danced around me and made it look as if I was supposed to just stand there. I didn't know what to do. But I had remembered that Rachel had told me that if I got too scared, just to smile and pretend I was enjoying myself. So, that's what I did. And eventually my brain believed that I was happy and I began to move. A little. Then more until I mirrored Rachel's movements. People thought I was supposed to be a doll that came to life, and Rachel never told them any different.

CHAPTER 16

"Mom," Olivia shouts. "Can I play the flute?"

"I'm in the basement," Elizabeth yells. "I can't hear you."

Olivia walks down the basement steps. Elizabeth looks up from the box she's packing with old Christmas decorations to take to the Goodwill store.

"Can I play the flute? Can I? Can I?"

"What in the world made you ask to play the flute?"

"We got this paper today in school about learning to play an instrument. If I play the flute, I can be in the band."

"And you think that you have enough time in your busy schedule to play the flute?"

Olivia nods.

"Let's talk about it tonight when Dad gets home."

Olivia sighs. "OK. But I really do want to play."

* * *

Grandma wanted me to play the violin. She had an old one that had been in her family for years. She took it to an instrument repair shop and struck a deal with the owner. He would put new strings on it, rehair the bow, and throw in a cake of resin and a chin rest. In exchange, Grandma would alter a couple pairs of pants that no longer fit him since he had a gastric bypass. Everyone was happy, most of all Grandma.

The teacher who directed the junior and high school orchestras gave lessons to third-graders who were just starting out. I was in a group with three other students. We met once a week during the afternoon recess in the music room.

My heart just wasn't into playing the violin. I wanted it to be. I wanted to make Grandma proud. I thought that if I played the violin and got really good at it that it would give Grandma something to brag about to the other ladies she worked with at the bridal shop where she did alterations. But I stunk.

"Sarah," Miss Wagaman said one day. "Can you stay after class for a minute? I'll write you a pass to return to your class."

I packed up my violin, taking my time so that the other kids had a chance to leave. I felt my face heat up. I thought Miss Wagaman was going to yell at me.

"Come, sit beside me."

I sat on the cold metal folding chair next to her.

"Do you like playing the violin?"

I looked down at the tan speckled floor streaked with black shoe marks. "My Grandma wants me to play. This violin has been in her family forever."

"That's not what I asked. Do *you* want to play?"

"Well, I practice all the time. Every day."

"Sarah, look at me."

I stopped looking at the floor and looked at Miss Wagaman.

"Do you want to play the violin?"

I bit my lower lip.

"Don't be afraid to tell me the truth. It's OK whatever the answer is. I won't be mad."

I shook my head no and started to cry. "But Grandma wants me to play and I don't want to disappoint her."

"It's OK, Sarah. Playing the violin isn't for everyone. Just like playing a sport isn't for everyone. Hopefully you'll find your passion one day and when you do, you won't practice because you're told to but because you want to. And there'll be a big difference in the outcome."

"How will I know what I'm good at?"

"By trying different things," Miss Wagaman said. "You tried the violin. You've tried for nearly a year now and it's not for you. And that's OK. So, maybe it's time to try something else. Not because your grandma wants you to or I want you to but because you want to."

"But how will I tell Grandma? I don't want her to be mad at me."

"Just tell her. Sometimes what we fear the most is what we should fear the least. Your grandma doesn't love you because you play the violin. She loves you for you. And, adults are pretty smart. They often have things figured out way before kids do."

"Was I really that bad?"

"I could just tell that your heart wasn't in it and I'd rather have you find something that your heart is in."

"What if I don't find anything?" I asked.

"You will. Life has a way of leading us down paths that we didn't know were there."

* * *

"Dad, Dad." Olivia runs to greet him at the door. "Can I play the flute?"

Tom looks at Elizabeth.

"Hey, Libs, let me at least get in the door."

Olivia follows her dad as he hangs up his overcoat, sits his leather briefcase in his office and grabs a cup of black coffee.

He pulls out a kitchen chair and sits down. "Now, what's this about the flute?"

"We got this paper today about playing an instrument. Emma's going to play the flute and I want to play the flute, too."

"Because Emma's doing it or because you want to do it?"

"Both."

"Do you think you have enough time to play the flute and dance?"

"Yes."

Tom looks at Elizabeth. "Remember last year when you wanted to play the viola and quit after a few weeks?"

Olivia nods. "But that was different."

"How so?"

"It made my arms tired and my chin hurt."

"What about the time you wanted to play basketball? And soccer?"

"I had to run too much."

"Here's the deal, Libs. Your mom and I want you to try new things. We understand it's part of growing up. Heck, I tried a lot of different things when I was a kid. But we don't want you to do something because your best friend is doing it. We want you to do it because you want to do it. Don't be a follower or feel pressured into doing something just because other people are doing it. And, I don't like you starting stuff and not finishing it. That's a bad habit to get into."

"Your dad's right, Libby."

"But I really want to play the flute."

"How about you think about it for a couple of days? If you still want to try it then, we'll talk about it again."

Olivia hangs her head. "OK."

* * *

I thought about my talk with Miss Wagaman the rest of the day. By the time I got home I had rehearsed my speech to Grandma so much that when I opened my mouth the words gushed out as if they had been held hostage and couldn't wait to be freed.

"Gram, I know how much you wanted me to play the violin because it's been in your family like forever but I stink at it and it's just not for me and I'm sorry because I want you to be proud of me even if I don't play the violin like you wanted me to."

"Sarah, slow down," Grandma said. "Come here and sit with me."

I followed Grandma to the couch. She eased herself down into the flattened cushion. I could tell that her knee was bothering her.

"Knee OK?"

"Just a little arthritis. Nothing to worry about. Now, let's talk about the violin."

"I stink at it and I wanted to be good at it for you but I don't like it and—"

"Stop, my sweet child," Grandma said. "First, it's true. I wanted you to play the violin, but I thought you wanted to play it, too. And, if you don't, you can stop. The last thing I want is for you to do something you really don't want to do because you think it's expected of you. If I told you to jump out our fifth-floor apartment window, would you?"

I shook my head no.

"I'm old, Sarah. I'm not going to be around forever."

"Don't say that."

"Well, it's true. You got to learn to make your own choices and not decide something based on what you think I want."

"But what if I make the wrong choice?" I asked.

"That's part of growing up. Heaven knows I've made plenty of wrong choices. But when you make a wrong choice, learn from it. If you fall, get up. That's what we Ross girls do. We keep going because it's all we can do. You can't go back and change the past, but you can learn from it and make better decisions in the future."

"So you're not mad?"

Grandma kissed the top of my head. "I'm not mad. And, I'll be honest, I'm not gonna miss that screeching. It gave me a headache. I think I've taken more aspirin this past year than I've taken my entire life. I happen to know the neighbors will be happy, too."

We both laughed and I realized that Miss Wagaman was right. Sometimes grown-ups are pretty smart. They figure things out way before kids do. And the things we fear aren't nearly as scary as we imagine them to be.

* * *

Elizabeth picks Olivia up after school to drive her to the dance studio. She's now in company at the dance academy, which means practices four times a week, a lot for a ten-year-old. Olivia eats the peanut butter and jelly sandwich Elizabeth has packed along with a yogurt. She decides to save the banana for later.

"How was school today?" Elizabeth asks.

"OK. Everyone was talking about being in the band."

"I see."

"Mom," Olivia says. "I don't think I want to play the flute after all."

Elizabeth glances at Olivia. "But just last night you wanted to. What changed your mind?"

"Well, I thought about what Dad said. About me always wanting to try all these different things and how I need to make sure it's what I want to do and not do it because everyone else is doing it."

"And?"

"And what I love most is dancing. So, I'm going to stick with dancing and work on it and be the best dancer I can be."

Elizabeth reaches over and squeezes Olivia's hand. "I'm so proud of you, Libby."

"You are?"

"Yes," Elizabeth says. "My little girl is growing up."

"That's a good thing, right?"

Elizabeth smiles. "It's a very good thing."

CHAPTER 17

Olivia drags her purple suitcase out of her walk-in closet that looks like a mini department store. She has so many clothes that you can't even see the racks they hang on. Boxes and boxes of shoes are stacked along the sides and purses of every sort spill out of a red plastic tub in the corner. The wire shelf that hugs the closet walls is packed with stacks of sweaters and sweatshirts and other clothes that didn't fit on the racks. It's piled high with so much stuff that the weight is making the bracket connecting the shelf to the wall come loose. I see the screw has worked its way out and I wonder if Olivia sees it.

Olivia looks at the list of things she's supposed to pack for the week-long dance camp she's attending in New York City. She's never spent more than two days away from her parents and she's worried about getting homesick.

She packs all of her dance gear and some shorts and tops.

Elizabeth walks in. "Don't forget your swimsuits. There's a pool at the complex."

Olivia sighs. "I'm going to need two suitcases. It's never all going to fit in one."

Elizabeth returns with a burgundy and black floral bag. It's one of the smaller pieces in her designer set. "Here, you can use this. All of your dance gear should fit in it and then you can use your suitcase for everything else."

Olivia removes the dance gear from the purple suitcase and puts it into the floral bag. "Did you go to camp when you were a kid?"

Elizabeth smiles. "Church camp."

"Was it fun?"

"Loads. And I'm sure you'll have fun, too."

"But what if I get homesick?"

"Libs," Elizabeth says. "You can call anytime you want. That's why we bought you a cell phone. And we'll be up at the end of the week to see the closing performance. You'll be just fine, sweetie."

"Sure?"

"Positive."

* * *

I went to church camp once and hated it. I got a full scholarship to go so it didn't cost Gram a dime. She thought I'd have a lot of fun. I didn't.

I had just gotten my period for the first time the day before I left. Even though Grandma had talked to me about it and I had read a book about it and saw a film in school, I freaked when I went to the bathroom and saw blood.

Grandma wasn't home at the time, and I didn't know where she put the "special stuff" she had bought for when the "big day" arrived. So I rolled toilet paper into a big ball and stuffed it in my underwear. Then I lay on my bed and cried until she came home.

"Sarah," Grandma called. "I'm home. Come and help me with the groceries."

I walked out to the kitchen.

"What's wrong?" Grandma asked. "You look like you've been crying."

I ran into Grandma's open arms and sobbed. She hugged me and kissed the top of my head. "Shh. Nothing can be that bad."

"I. I. I got that thing you said I would get."

Grandma pulled back so I was at arm's length and she could see my blotchy face and looked me in the eyes. "Your period? You got your period?"

I nodded.

"Oh, sweet child," Grandma said. "It's OK. It's just part of growing up. Did you find the stuff I bought?"

"I couldn't remember where you put it."

"It's in the bathroom in a box on the bottom shelf."

I went to the bathroom, found the box, pulled out the wad of toilet paper and unwrapped a maxi-pad. Grandma tried to show me how to use a tampon later that night, but it was no use. It hurt too much.

"Take them along just in case," Grandma said. "You can't swim unless you can get one of these in you."

My luck I happened to go to church camp the hottest week of the summer. It was a blistering ninety-three degrees most days and everyone spent as much time as possible in the cool pool fed by a nearby spring. And, of course, they couldn't understand why I didn't want to go swimming. I gave them a million excuses. I think the girls knew the real reason, but the boys were totally clueless.

So while they were swimming, I was under a shady weeping willow reading. It was the most miserable week of my life.

* * *

Olivia spends her days shuffling from one air-conditioned studio to another. She studies hip hop, jazz, Broadway and lyrical dance, rotating between the studios and instructors. At night, she participates in team competitions, like team cheers or dance trivia, or individual competitions, such as the Dance Idol night.

"Hi, Mom," she says when she calls the first night. "How's Daisy?"

"Missing you. She's been looking all over the house for you. How's it going?" Elizabeth asks.

"OK. I miss Daisy, too. And you and Dad."

"Have you made any friends?" Elizabeth asks.

"Not really. The girls here aren't like the girls at home."

"What do you mean, Lib?"

"I don't know. They're just different. And a lot of them have been attending this camp for the past few summers so they've been friends for a while."

"So you're the new girl, huh?" Elizabeth asks.

"Yes. I guess that's it. Just feeling a little left out. And I overheard one of the girls making fun of my bag."

"The one I gave you for your dance stuff?"

"Yes," Olivia says. "She called it a Grandma bag."

"Hang in there, Lib," Elizabeth says. "Being away on your own without any friends isn't easy. But just be yourself, and you can call me anytime."

"Thanks, Mom," Olivia says. "I did learn some new moves today. And I'm about ready to leave to go to flexibility, strength and leaps night. And I'm excited about that."

"Great. I hope you have fun and I can't wait for you to show me everything you've learned."

"Is Dad home?" Olivia asks.

"He's working late, but I'll tell him you called."

"Tell him that I love him and I'll talk to him soon. Oh, and tell him I loved his surprise."

"Surprise?" Elizabeth asks.

"Yeah. There was a special delivery waiting for me when I got here. It was a box filled with my favorite snacks and a huge stuffed ballerina bear that said princess on it."

"That's your dad," Elizabeth says. "I'll tell him. Love you."

"Love you, too."

* * *

Ever since I've recorded Olivia's moments, I've noticed that her family is never stingy with the "I love you"s or hugs and kisses. In fact, they might go a bit overboard. I've never been around a family that is so demonstrative. I know that Grandma loved me, but even she didn't say it as much as Olivia's parents say it. Nor as much as Olivia's grandparents say it or as much as her aunts and uncles say it. It seems like everyone is in love with everyone else to the nth degree. There is so much love in this family that it reminds me of how little I had.

I remember the time Grandma found my diary and read it. I was at the kitchen table doing homework when she walked in.

"Do you really feel this way, Sarah?"

I looked up. She was holding my black houndstooth diary.

"Well, do you?"

I stood up. "I can't believe you read my diary."

"It's not like I went looking for it. It was open on your bed. I went to take off your bed sheets to wash them. I had to pick it up."

"You didn't have to read it."

"Well, I did. Is this how you feel?"

"I was angry when I wrote that."

"Angry about what?"

"You grounded me."

"I grounded you because you lied about not going to school. And I will ground you again if you ever lie to me again. I've told you over and over that the worst thing you can do is lie to me. But, that doesn't mean I don't love you."

I looked down at the red brick linoleum floor. I knew what I wrote would hurt Grandma. Deep inside, I wanted to punish her for grounding me. Make her feel like crap. And, I purposely left the diary on my bed hoping she would find it and read it. Looking back, I was immature. I knew that a surefire way to hurt Grandma was to write that she didn't love me. I knew that it would be like stabbing her in the heart. What is it about teenage angst that makes us do such horrible things to those we love?

* * *

Olivia and the other dancers dress for their big show. Olivia peeks out from the left stage wing. A steady stream of parents and siblings and grandparents walk through the back doors, program in hand, looking for seats.

The final performance at the end of the week always draws a crowd. The dancers get a chance to show off the new skills and routines they've learned throughout the week.

Olivia is about to perform her first dance. Her modern dance instructor introduces the piece, explaining the origins of modern dance and the influence of such great dancers and choreographers as Martha Graham.

Olivia enters the stage barefoot, wearing a simple black Lycra jumpsuit. I know how much Olivia loves modern dance. Even though she's not yet a teen, she understands how to connect with her innermost emotions and how to convey these emotions through movement and expression.

All week, her dance instructor has challenged her to get in touch with an emotion, to choose a subject close to her heart. Olivia has. She hasn't told anyone what it is, but I know.

She's chosen abandonment, a feeling she would never share with her parents. But she's never quite understood why her birth parents didn't want her. There's an aching deep in her heart that longs for answers to questions she's too afraid to ask.

When the melancholy music starts, Olivia begins. Her movements marry the music. She bends and twists and throws herself on the stage in despair. The sophistication of her dance surprises everyone, even the instructor, who notices that Olivia has incorporated some new moves she's never seen before. When she's done, the crowd stands and applauds. They know they've just witnessed something special.

* * *

Like Olivia, I had questions, too. I never felt abandoned, but I always longed for love. I had Grandma's love but I wanted more. I wanted more people to love me, to really care about me. It was like being thirsty and never getting enough water to quench your thirst. That was how I felt about love. I had some, but never enough. So, if I were to choose an emotion to focus on in a modern dance, I'd choose desperate for love.

* * *

When Olivia gets home from dance camp, there's a surprise waiting for her.

"Close your eyes until I tell you to open them," says Elizabeth, holding onto Olivia's arm and guiding her down the hall toward her bedroom.

Tom waits with the video camera inside Olivia's room. He wants to capture her reaction. While Olivia was away at camp, they hired a designer to completely redo her bedroom, changing it from a little girl's room into a teen's.

"OK. Now."

Olivia opens her eyes. Her hands cup her mouth and her eyes start to water.

She walks inside and turns one hundred and eighty degrees. The brown and blue tones add sophistication to what has become a contemporary space. There's a sitting area with a brown sofa, flanked by blue chairs. A flatscreen TV is mounted on the facing wall. The bedroom furniture is all new – the white of her childhood replaced with a rich cherry. The four-poster bed is draped in a sheer fabric.

Elizabeth notices Olivia's expression. Olivia looks as if she's about to cry, but it's not the type of cry that comes from being happy. It's more like the type of cry that comes from being upset.

Tom is still recording Olivia.

"Dad and I thought that it was about time you had a more grown-up room, a space where you could also hang out with your friends," Elizabeth explains.

"What did you do with my old furniture?" asks Olivia, her lips trembling.

"Donated it to charity."

"But I didn't want new furniture. I liked my old furniture."

"We thought some little girl would get some use out of it."

"But, but I thought you were going to let me do this?"

Tom stops recording. "Don't you like it, Lib?"

"Yes. It's great. But that's not the point," Olivia says. "We talked about this and you were going to let me redo my room. Now it's all done the way you wanted to do it, not the way I wanted to do it."

Elizabeth and Tom look stunned. They thought Olivia would be happy. It never occurred to them that she wouldn't be.

* * *

One night Grandma came home with a new bedspread. She found it at Goodwill and it had never been opened. It was a black and white zebra stripes trimmed in hot pink. It was the coolest bedspread I had ever seen. The tag said Pottery Barn.

"Oh, Gram, I love it."

"Thought it was about time to get rid of that ratty Barbie bedspread," Grandma said. "That thing's so old it's threadbare in spots."

Grandma never knew it, but I looked the bedspread up online. There were tons of accessories you could buy to go with it. A switch plate. Lampshade. Pillows. Rug.

I imagined what my room would look like if I had all of those things. I thought it would be the coolest teen room ever.

But the bedspread was as close as I got to a bedroom makeover. Even so, I thought I was probably the happiest kid in the world.

CHAPTER 18

"What are you girls giggling about?" Elizabeth asks.

Olivia and Emma are in the back seat texting each other. They are going to the junior high dance.

Elizabeth stops at a red light and glances back. "Are you texting each other because you don't want me to know what you're talking about?"

The girls each flash a mouth full of braces with pink rubber bands and wires.

"Well, it's secret stuff," Olivia says.

"Yeah, Mrs. K. Secret stuff," Emma says.

"There was a time when you two told me everything. Guess those days are coming to an end."

They pull into the school parking lot and join the line of cars crawling to the front door to drop kids off.

"Remember," Elizabeth says. "Dad will pick you up at nine unless you call and want picking up earlier."

The girls giggle again.

"Thanks, Mom," Olivia says. "And thanks for the new outfit."

"Have fun," Elizabeth says. "And remember what we talked about. No risqué dancing. If other kids want to dance like that, let them. But you better not."

"They're cracking down on that, Mrs. K," Emma says. "Principal said that if anyone's caught dirty dancing they'll be thrown out and their parents will be called to come and get them."

"About time they do something about that," Elizabeth says. "Parents were complaining about the way kids dance at the PTO meeting the other night."

* * *

I'll never forget the one and only junior high school dance I went to. Rachel talked me into it. I would have rather stayed home and rented movies as we normally did on weekends. But, Rachel really wanted to go so I agreed.

The night started out bad. I forgot my school ID and it was a hassle getting in the door. One teacher had to get another teacher who had to get another teacher before I was cleared. And then when Rachel and I walked into the school cafeteria, which had been transformed into a Winter Wonderland with giant snowflakes dangling from the ceiling and fake snow everywhere, we got the stare down from Tracey Carmichael and her minions.

"Don't look now, but Tracey's headed this way," I told Rachel. "And Tara and Paige are with her."

"Hi, girls," Tracey said. "Do you like what we did to the cafeteria?"

Tracey was on student council and headed the social committee, which planned all of the dances.

"It looks nice," I said.

"Yeah, nice job," Rachel said.

Tracey looked me straight in the eyes. "Are you going to dance tonight?"

"Probably not," I said.

"Well, that's a good thing," Tracey said. "You're one of the clumsiest people I know."

Tara and Paige giggled.

Tracey scanned my clothes from my black shirt with silver and white sequins around the V-neckline to my black jeans. "Remember the time, girls, that little Miss I-get-my-clothes-at-Goodwill tried to turn on the balance beam and slipped and fell off and sprained her ankle?"

They all giggled except Rachel. I stared at the cafeteria floor and prayed that I would melt away like Frosty when he got trapped in that greenhouse. No one would miss me, I thought. Well, maybe Grandma and Rachel. But no one else – especially Tracey. She hated my guts all of my life and I had no idea why. Grandma said Tracey was jealous, but I never understood why. She had everything I didn't.

"Come on, Sarah," Rachel said. "Let's get a drink."

We walked away from Tracey, Tara and Paige, but their giggles hung in the air like whole notes.

"I told you I didn't want to come," I told Rachel. "I hate Tracey Carmichael. I hate how she always makes me feel. Like I'm a piece of crap. Crap. Crap. Crap."

"Listen, Sarah," Rachel said. "You let her make you feel like crap. Don't. You've got to learn to stand up for yourself, otherwise, she'll just keep whacking you every chance she gets."

"No, she won't, because I won't come to any more stupid dances."

"It might not be at a dance. It might be in the hallway or during gym class or outside of school somewhere. Like the mall. You're an easy target because you just take it and she knows that and uses that to her advantage. Don't let her."

"I just don't know why she hates me so much."

"You really don't know why?" Rachel asked.

"No. She's hated me for as long as I can remember."

"It's because you're drop-dead gorgeous. Always have been. And you don't need any make-up or anything. You're what my mom calls a natural beauty."

"I don't feel pretty."

"But you are and for people like Tracey who have to work hard at being pretty, they resent people like you who don't have to do anything."

"But you're pretty and she's never treated you the way she treats me."

"In case you haven't noticed, I'm black in a school that's mostly white. I had cornrows growing up until I pleaded with my mom to let me straighten my hair this year. I've never been any competition for Tracey Carmichael. But you, you outshine her and you don't even realize it or care. And that's what burns her up."

That night, with Rachel's help, I was braver than I'd ever been. Rachel and I danced and people actually stopped to watch. No one had any idea that Rachel had given me dance lessons for months. My hard work had paid off. It was as if all of the snowflakes were aligned and no one, not even Tracey Carmichael, could melt them. I wasn't clumsy. I didn't fall. I danced as I had never danced before.

* * *

Olivia and Emma join their friends on the dance floor in front of where the DJ is set up. Huge speakers sit on the floor beside his table and are so loud that it's impossible to hear anyone talk. Olivia lassoes the song's pulse-thumping tempo and it's as if her body has awakened from a winter slumber. She moves without thinking.

Leaps.

Jumps.

Turns.

Falls.

She uses her body and the space around her to express herself. The others catch her moves and fall back one after another to form a circle around her. Even at a junior high school dance her moves command attention. The kids in the circle clap and shout and more kids dribble over to see what all the commotion is about.

Olivia doesn't realize she's in the spotlight. She's married to the music, oblivious to everything but the burning tempo. Her heart races and I know that she's found her passion. It's only when the song stops that she realizes that she's dancing alone. Everyone breaks out in a thunderous applause and Olivia backs away from the center to join Emma.

"Why didn't you stop me?" she asks Emma.

"Because I loved watching you," Emma says. "We all did. You really got something special there, Lib. No one can dance like you."

Olivia is embarrassed by the attention her dancing has brought. The rest of the night, girls and boys comment on her dance moves. She tries to blend in with the crowd but it's clear that her dancing has set her apart.

"Dad just texted me," Olivia tells Emma. "He's out front. Are you ready?"

The girls say goodbye to their friends and as they're walking out the door, an eighth-grader with dreads approaches.

"I saw you dancing earlier," he says. "You're good."

"Thanks," Olivia says.

"I dance, too. Maybe we can get together and dance sometime."

"Maybe."

He flashes a gummy smile that shows his bright white teeth. "Later."

"Yeah, see ya," Olivia says.

"Oh. My. Gawd. Terrell Jackson talked to you."

"Terrell who?" Olivia asks.

"He's just one of the most popular boys in eighth grade," Emma said. "Great football player."

"How do you know these things?"

"Well, this girl in my Sunday school class likes him big time. She's in eighth grade, too. She's always talking about him to another girl in the class. I sit right beside her so it's hard not to hear."

The girls find Olivia's dad's car and slip in the back.

"Have fun?" Tom asks.

"Loads," Olivia says.

"Dance with any boys?"

Olivia rolls her eyes. "No, Dad. I only danced one dance and it was fast and there were a lot of people on the dance floor."

Tom smiles.

"But," Emma says, "Libby's one dance was the talk of the night. An eighth-grader even asked her to dance with him sometime."

"Eighth-grader? Isn't that a little old?"

"It's one year, Dad. You're four years older than Mom."

"True," Tom says. "But I was a lot older when I met your mom. Four years when you're twenty-six is different than four years when you're twelve."

"Well, I'll soon be thirteen."

"Yes, I know," Tom says. "You keep reminding me that you'll soon be a teen."

CHAPTER 19

Emma and Olivia are in Olivia's bedroom. Magazines are scattered on the bed. The girls look through the glossy magazines, commenting on the fashions and hairstyles of the models.

"I like her hair," says Olivia, showing the page to Emma.

"I don't like the bangs," Emma says.

"But bangs are in."

"Still, not for me. What about this one?"

Emma flips her magazine over so Olivia can see the picture of a girl with stick-straight hair cut on an angle.

"I would never be able to get away with that," says Olivia, shaking her curls. "Remember that time you straightened my hair with your flat iron?"

Emma laughs. "Yeah, it curled up at the ends. I couldn't get it to stay straight."

"Do you think I have a big nose?" asks Olivia, changing the subject before Emma has a chance to finish her thought.

"No. Do I?"

"No," Olivia says.

"What about my ears?"

"Your ears are fine. Mine are pointy," Olivia says.

"Just a little, but they're cute. And your ears are attached to the side of your head. Not like mine, which dangle. I'd rather have attached lobes like you."

Olivia feels her earlobes. "Never noticed that before. You're weird."

"Not any weirder than you."

The girls laugh.

* * *

Watching Olivia and Emma becoming teens makes me happy and sad at the same time. Now I know how Grandma must have felt when I was growing up. One day Olivia was playing with dolls and the next day she's putting on makeup and thinking about boys. I know that I'm just her moment keeper but I can't help worrying about her. She's getting older and her parents have less and less control over her life. I want her to make good decisions, and yet I know from experience that not all of the decisions she'll make will be good ones.

I remember the speech Grandma gave me about making choices. I was around thirteen.

"It's like driving a car," Grandma said. "You come to an intersection and you got to decide which way you're gonna go. Right, left or straight. And no matter which way you choose, you'll have to deal with what lies ahead. Sometimes there's a pothole. I hate those. Or a tree that fell during a bad storm. Doesn't matter what's blocking your way, you got to figure out how to get around it. I'm not saying it's easy. And it's definitely not fun, but it will make you stronger and wiser. Why, look at me. I had so many trees fall in my life that I was beginning to think I wasn't supposed to keep going. Turned out those trees helped me build one heck of a fire that couldn't be doused by misfortune and bad luck. After all, I got you."

Guess I had forgotten this speech when I decided to kill myself. Guess I allowed the pothole to become a sinkhole and swallow me whole. Grandma wouldn't have been proud.

* * *

Emma looks into Olivia's mirror. "I think I'm getting a zit."

Olivia gets up. "Let me see."

Emma sticks out her chin. She points to it with her finger. "Right there. See?"

"Yeah, I see it."

"Think I should pop it?"

"No. Mom says that's bad. Here, you can use this cream she bought me. It dries zits up and conceals them at the same time."

"Hey, want to make each other up?"

Olivia nods. "My grandma bought me this new professional makeup kit. It's got loads of stuff. Something like forty eye shadows, several bronzers and blushers, two eyeliners and lots of lip colors."

Olivia gets the kit and returns. "Do you want to go first?"

Emma nods.

"Let's do it in my bathroom. The lighting's better."

Emma follows Olivia into her bathroom and sits on the chair at the built-in vanity. Olivia hands her a headband to keep her hair off of her face, then she starts applying the foundation.

"Good thing we're the same skin tone," Olivia says.

I watch as Olivia applies the makeup and it reminds me of when she was little and played with her Mattel doll bust. She'd spend hours combing and braiding and twisting the doll's hair and applying makeup.

Olivia smiles. "OK. Open your eyes."

Emma opens her eyes and turns to look in the mirror. "Wow! You're good at this."

"So you like it?"

"Love it. Now your turn."

The only makeup I've ever worn was mascara. I didn't like the feeling of having stuff on my face. Especially when I was hot and sweaty. I imagined it melting into my pores and my face breaking out and looking like a pepperoni pizza. That's what Tracey Carmichael called this one girl in our class. Peyton was plagued with zits. And she picked them so it made her face look worse.

"Hey, look who's coming," Tracey yelled one day in the hallway. "It's pizza girl."

I watched as Peyton hung her head and walked past Tracey. Everyone laughed.

"Hey, Peyton. Wait up?" I ran to catch up to her.

She stopped.

"Don't let that jerk get to you," I said.

"Easy for you to say. Your skin's perfect. Your life's perfect. Mine sucks."

Later that day, I heard that Peyton had found a picture of a pizza that was cut out of a magazine taped to her locker. She never did come back to school after that. And I never could eat pizza without thinking about Peyton and how mean Tracey Carmichael was.

* * *

Olivia closes her eyes and Emma applies the eyeliner just above the lashes, starting from the inside corner and moving to the outside corner. She then lines the lower eyelid, moving from the outside edge in.

I watch as Olivia is transformed into a young woman. I prefer the no-makeup Olivia.

"OK. I think I'm done," Emma says.

Olivia opens her eyes and looks in the mirror. "You're good at this, too."

Olivia gets up. "Let's get my mom to take a picture of us."

She grabs her cell phone and runs to find her mom, who is in her office doing paperwork.

"Mom, can you take our picture?"

Elizabeth looks up and takes off her red reading glasses. "Wow! Don't you two look grown up."

"Well, we're just about thirteen," Olivia says.

"Please," Elizabeth says. "Don't remind me."

Elizabeth takes several pictures of the girls, some together and some separate. Afterward, they look at them on Olivia's phone.

Elizabeth points to one she had taken of Olivia holding Daisy. "Email me this one, Lib. I want to use it for my screensaver."

* * *

When I turned thirteen, Grandma brought home Chinese food to celebrate. Take-out was a rare treat at our house. It was the first time I used chopsticks – and the last! I never could get the hang of it. Neither could Grandma, but we had fun trying.

"What'd you get?" I asked Grandma as she lugged a brown bag into the apartment.

"A special meal for a special young lady," Grandma said. "Let's see here."

Grandma removed one item at a time from the bag. "I got won-ton soup. Egg rolls. Chicken and broccoli."

She winks at me. "That's my favorite. And pork fried rice. Oh, and for dessert, a fortune cookie."

I smiled. Grandma always made me feel special. We had so much that night eating Chinese and we had plenty of leftovers for the next day. I kept my cookie fortune for the longest time in my purse. Every time I got a new purse, I'd make sure I transferred the fortune to it. I carried it around as if it were a contract. As if it were something that was owed to me and I was holding onto it until it happened.

Every now and then I'd get it out and read it, wishing as hard as I could that the fortune were right. It said: Your dreams will come true.

But some dreams don't come true. Some dreams are like the little white strips of paper they're written on. They fade and become wrinkled, torn and tattered and are eventually thrown away. Paper dreams are like that. They sound good on paper, but that's all they ever are. In the end, they're trash like everything else.

CHAPTER 20

Olivia's in her bedroom on her phone. When she isn't at the dance studio or with Emma, that's what she's doing. Daisy's chewing on a plastic squeaky toy on the floor beside her. When Olivia's home, Daisy's never far from her side.

"Libby," Elizabeth calls from the bottom of the stairs. "Come here."

Olivia walks downstairs and sees her mom waving a piece of white paper.

"We got your interim grade report today in the mail, and I'm not happy."

Olivia's left eye and thumb twitch. She knows she's in trouble, especially since she got zeroes because she didn't hand in a couple of assignments.

Olivia follows her mom into the kitchen and plops on a wooden stool.

"Lib," Elizabeth says. "I'm really disappointed in this report. You got zeros in math class because you didn't hand in work. That's totally unacceptable."

"But I—"

"No. There are no excuses for not doing your work. Up until now, I haven't been checking your grades online. That changes today. From now on, I will check every day. I will see the grade for every assignment, every test in every class. I want to see these grades improve and improve significantly."

"But I hate math. It's hard. And I'm really not crazy about science either."

"Well, you can't major in socializing in college. Right now, you're in junior high and these grades won't matter like the ones in high school will when you apply to colleges. But you have to establish good study habits now so that when you get to high school, you'll be prepared to handle a much more rigorous workload. If you need help with math or science, ask for help. If Dad or I can't help you, we'll find someone who can."

"OK. But do you have to check my grades online?"

"Yes. But I'll make a deal with you. If you bring these grades up to where I think they should be and maintain them, I'll stop checking every day."

"Cause you'll make me nervous if you check every day and freak out over one little score. Kind of like what you and Dad are always telling me about looking at the bigger picture. If I have a bad day and get a bad score and you flip out, that's just going to make me more nervous and it could be that that one bad score isn't enough to mess up the overall score."

"Like I said, I'll stop checking every day when you bring these grades up. Bs or better. If you have to stay after school to get extra help, you can do that and I'll pick you up. In the meantime, lay off the cell phone. I don't understand why you have to text or talk to your friends all night when you've seen them in school all day anyhow."

"But it's not like we're talking all day in school, Mom."

"Well, you don't have all night to talk either because you have homework to do. Between school work and dance, I'd say you're a very busy girl with little time to waste chatting or texting."

"Did you tell Dad?"

"No, not yet. But I will and he might talk to you about it, too. Do you have homework tonight?"

Olivia nods.

"Then get it done. And if you need help, ask me."

Olivia slides off the stool and, with her head hanging, heads to her room. She has a test tomorrow and she knows she has to study, especially since her mom will be checking her grades online.

* * *

Unlike Olivia, I loved math. It was the one thing I was good at. And I liked it because there was only one correct answer. It was black and white; no gradients. Unlike English where if you were a good bullshitter, and I wasn't, you could write something and make it sound as if it were the greatest thing ever. Lots of gray in essays and totally subjective. Math? You either got it right or you didn't. I like the straightforwardness of the subject. No bullshit.

Whenever we had to take the state assessment tests, I always scored advanced in the math modules but below average in the English ones. I sucked at grammar. I never understood what the big deal was if I said "good" and I should have said "well". It's not as if there were grammar police that would arrest me if I used the wrong word when I got older.

I remember the time I left a poem I had written for class on the kitchen counter and Grandma found it.

He

He hated me.

He resented that I lived and my mom died.

He never called me by my first name. (I was "she" or "her" or "that kid" or "that girl". Never "Sarah".)

He was a drunk.

He was a freeloader.

He was an abusive jerk.

He was Matt.

Never my dad.

And now he's dead.

I'm glad.

Grandma looked up from the piece of paper. Tears slid down her saggy cheeks and she grabbed some tissues from the box in front of her.

"I'm sorry, Gram. You weren't supposed to see that."

Grandma pulled out the metal kitchen chair and held onto the table as she eased herself down. "I didn't know he had hurt you this much, that you felt this way. That you realized as much as you did. I thought you were just a kid and that you'd forget."

"You don't forget that the guy who is supposed to be your dad can't even say your name."

"He couldn't help it, Sarah. He was just too messed up after your mom died."

"Yes, he could have helped it, Gram. And he could have helped me. Stop making excuses for him. He was a drunk and a lazy ass and, if you ask me, not much of a son. He took from you and what you didn't give, he stole."

I had never said such horrible things about Matt to Grandma and I felt bad that I had made her cry. Grandma was the last person I'd ever want to hurt.

"Who's seen this?" Grandma asked.

"My teacher."

"Anyone else?"

I shook my head. "But I don't care if anyone else does. It's how I feel. The only thing I'm sorry about is that you found it."

"I know it's your poem, Sarah. You have a right to write it and a right to feel the way you do. But I'm going to ask you something. Can you please not share this with anyone else? At least till after I'm gone."

I nodded. "But it's not a reflection on you, Gram. It's not your fault Matt turned out the way he did. You're always telling me that people have choices and that the choices they make determine what kind of life they lead. Matt made his choices; you didn't make them for him."

Grandma took a deep breath. "Can you help me up the stairs?"

I walked over and helped Gram off the chair and to her room.

"I'm tired, Sarah," Grandma said. "And all I want to do is sleep."

*   *   *

"Lib," Elizabeth calls. "Dinner's ready."

Olivia runs down the steps.

"Walk!" her mom yells. "You sound like a herd of cattle coming down those steps."

Olivia slows to a walk and enters the kitchen. "Where's Dad?"

"He just called. He's working late so we're going to eat without him. Can you grab the Parmesan cheese from the fridge?"

Olivia opens the refrigerator and grabs the green can of cheese from the side door. She turns around. "Did you tell him about the grade report?"

"Not yet," says Elizabeth, looking up from setting the table. "Do you want to?"

Olivia shakes her head.

"How's the studying going, anyway?" Elizabeth asks.

"OK. I hate word problems, though. I like words on their own, but I don't like it when they're mixed with numbers. It confuses me."

"If you need help after dinner, let me know. It's been a long time since I've done word problems, but I could probably figure it out."

"Did you like math when you were in school?" Olivia asks her mom.

"Not as much as science, but I did well in it."

"Were you popular?"

"Not like you," Elizabeth says. "You're involved in so many things and have so many friends. I was an Army brat and we moved a lot. Never stayed in one place long enough to make any really good friends, like you and Emma."

Olivia twists the spaghetti around her fork. "I wouldn't like that. I couldn't imagine not having Emma to talk to."

"You're lucky," Elizabeth says. "Some people have no one."

* * *

Elizabeth is right about that. Rachel moved when we were in junior high. She was the only friend I ever had. When she moved, it was as if someone put a veil over the sun. Life was never as bright and when bad things happened, the darkness seemed darker.

I wasn't popular like Olivia and I wasn't involved in all of the things she's involved in. After Rachel moved, I just kept to myself. Was easier that way.

Didn't have to explain why I lived with Gram. I heard their whispers from time to time, mostly mocking my clothes. And when the middle school French teacher commented in class that I could be a model, I thought Tracey Carmichael and the other girls were going to explode.

If their looks could kill, I would have been dead a hundred times that day. And that was the day when things got worse in school. The day their whispers became black whipping tongues, taunting me and lashing out every chance they got.

"Did anyone ever tell you that you should be a model?" Miss Murphy said.

She was looking at me but I thought she was talking to the student behind me. I turned around and there was a boy in that chair.

"I'm talking to you, Sarah," Miss Murphy said.

My hand slapped my chest. "Me? Uh, no. No one has ever said that."

"Well, you should think about it. I have a friend who's involved with a local agency. If you want, I can give you her business card."

I could feel the burning eyes of every girl in the class. Rachel always said I was a "natural beauty" but I never thought I was anything special. I didn't wear designer clothes or go to a salon to have my hair done.

Gram still set up a makeshift salon in the kitchen, spreading an old shower curtain on the linoleum floor and putting one of the kitchen chairs in the middle. She'd been cutting my hair ever since I had hair to cut. It was all I knew and it seemed to work OK for me. Plus it saved money. That was the real reason Gram cut it. It was also the reason why she stopped getting perms. She figured the money she spent on perms she could spend on me. Especially now that I was older. I needed more girl stuff – like tampons and deodorant and shaving cream.

After class, Miss Murphy gave me her friend's business card. I didn't want to take it. I knew that Tracey and the others were watching.

Miss Murphy shook the card in her hand. "Here, take it. At least think about it."

I took the card and looked down at the floor and walked out the door, past Tracey and the others. And I threw that card away at the first trash can I came to making sure that Tracey saw me. But it didn't do any good. I was labeled pretty and there was no one who was going to be labeled pretty in the whole junior high but Tracey Carmichael.

CHAPTER 21

"I can't decide on a theme for my locker," Olivia tells Emma. They're hanging out in Olivia's bedroom, painting their nails with the new polish they bought at the mall earlier in the day.

"I thought you'd choose dance like last year," Emma says.

"Yeah, but that's so expected. Of course I would choose dance because it's my favorite thing in the entire universe. But, I was thinking about doing something unexpected. Like maybe focus on a particular color. Like pink or purple or blue and brown like my bedroom. What about you?"

"Think I'll pick Tink. She's my all-time favorite Disney character and I've seen lots of Tink stuff in stores."

"Tink is good."

"You don't think it's too babyish?" Emma asks.

"Nah! You're never too old for Tink. My grandma even has a Tink sweatshirt."

Last year was the first year the girls decorated the inside of their lockers. It turned into quite a competition in their eighth-grade wing. The school allowed them to decorate as long as they used materials that could easily be removed and didn't damage the surface or leave a sticky residue.

Most of the girls got really creative. One girl made a mailbox by mounting a decorated tissue box on the inside of her locker door below the slits. Friends could "mail" notes whenever they wanted. Olivia thought that was the coolest idea ever.

Of course there were the usual magnetic mirrors and photo frames and pen and pencil holders and whiteboards. And most everyone hung a string of battery operated lights. And some sort of air freshener was a must.

"What about a tropical theme?" Olivia asks. "I have tons of photos from our trip to Hawaii."

"And leis," Emma says.

Olivia smiles. "Yeah, lots of those."

"That could definitely work."

"Or maybe a Hollywood theme, like glitz and glam," says Olivia, tightening the cap on her Outta Sight Orange polish. "I know. I could make the inside of the locker look like a strip of film and get photos enlarged to fit in the spaces. Maybe it could be my life in film and I could include dance photos."

"I like it," Emma says. "What's the name of that black board with the white lines they snap when they make movies?"

"That's a clapboard," Olivia says. "I don't think I'd have room for a full-size one, but I'm sure I can think of some way to incorporate it. Maybe I can find a plastic thumb, glue a magnet to the back of it. Then, depending on what kind of day I'm having, I can turn it up for thumbs up or down for thumbs down. Like the movie reviewers do."

"You're definitely on a roll with this," Emma says. "I like it."

Olivia and Emma continue to discuss locker décor, coming up with ideas for their friends who might need some help. They decide that Robin, a forward on the basketball team, should mount a Nerf basketball net on the inside of her locker door and that Becca, who's in chorus, could line her locker with sheet music.

* * *

My locker was of the standard drab gray variety. The bottom was rusty so I threw in an old towel to protect my books. That was as far as I went with my locker overhaul, and that was mostly because I didn't want to be charged for damaging my books at the end of the year when the teachers collected them. I wasn't one of those girls who turned the back of their locker door into a photo gallery. It was definitely not a place I wanted to spend any time at or any money on. Its only purpose as far as I was concerned was to hold books so I didn't have to lug them to every class. And, after what happened the one day in ninth grade, I definitely didn't even like having to use it for that.

It was after lunch and I came back to my locker to get the books I needed for my afternoon classes.

When I walked past Tracey Carmichael's huddle, I heard the usual whispers and felt their eyes follow me. When I reached my locker, I saw why.

Taped to my locker was a poster of me with letters cut out of a magazine that said: Fat Slut.

I turned toward Tracey's group. They were all laughing. I tore off the poster and ran to the bathroom. A few minutes later, Tracey and two of her friends walked in. I think the others guarded the door in case a teacher came.

Tracey banged on the stall. "Just remember, Goodwill Girl, you're a nobody. Not only are you fat, you're also ugly."

The other girls laughed.

"Real ugly. In fact, you're so ugly that your mama diapered your face, thinking it was your ass."

The girls laughed even louder.

"Oh, that's right. You don't have a mama. I forgot."

"Leave me alone," I cried.

"Sure, bitch. But stay out of my way."

I hated Tracey and her friends. I hated Rachel for moving and leaving me alone. And I hated myself for not punching that bitch in the face as I wanted to.

When the French teacher paid me that compliment, it was as if she taped a bull's-eye to my back. I was Tracey's personal target.

* * *

"Did you decide what you're going to wear on the first day?" Olivia asks Emma.

"I was going to wear the mini jean skirt and the pink tie-dyed shirt I bought last week but I kind of like the new dress I got today."

"Tough decision," Olivia says. "You look great in both."

"I can't believe we're starting high school," Emma says.

"Me neither."

"Do you think the older guys will be hot?"

Olivia rolls her eyes. "Totally."

"Think they'll look at us?"

"Maybe. But Mom and Dad said I can't date anyone who's older," Olivia says.

"They have to be in our grade?" Emma asks.

"Yeah."

"That's so lame."

"Tell me about it."

"If an older guy does ask you out," Emma says, "you could just lie and tell your parents he's your age."

Olivia doesn't say anything. She's never lied to her parents and she's not sure she ever would.

* * *

I used to tell Grandma little white lies all the time, mostly because I didn't want to make her feel bad or hurt her feelings. Like I'd tell her I was happy when I wasn't. That sort of thing.

"You need to smile more often," Grandma told me one Sunday after church. "People are always asking me if you're all right. 'Why doesn't that Sarah smile more?' they ask."

I shrugged my boney shoulders.

"Sarah," Grandma said. "What's wrong?"

"Nothing."

"Is it something I did? Something I didn't do?"

"No, Gram. You do everything right. I'm fine. Honest."

I wanted to tell Grandma how alone I felt, but I didn't want to hurt her feelings. I knew that she loved me and wanted me, but I was getting older and wanted someone else to love me and want me. A boy, perhaps. Only no boys ever looked my way. And if they did, they looked past me for whoever was behind me. Until. Well, that's a moment for later.

* * *

"Gretchen at church told me that girls should never go out with someone younger," Olivia tells Emma. "She says it's uncool."

"You mean like a senior girl dating a freshman guy?" Emma asks.

"Yeah. But it's totally cool and acceptable for a senior guy to date a freshman girl."

Emma scratches her head. "So it's OK for guys to date younger girls but it's not OK for girls to date younger guys."

"You got it," Olivia says. "According to Gretchen, who seems to know everything there is to know about guys."

"What about dating someone in your own grade?" Emma asks.

"Gretchen didn't say anything about that, so I guess it's OK."

As I listen to Olivia and Emma discuss the dos and don'ts of high school, I notice that some things haven't changed. The caste system is pretty much the same, with cheerleaders — like Emma — and jocks at the top and honor students — like Olivia — if they're cool and not nerdy; band geeks and drama and choir types in the middle; and the rejects at the bottom.

"Did you hear about Will Meade's dad?" Emma asks Olivia.

Olivia shakes her head.

"He was having an affair with the nanny and Will's mom caught them. Naked. In bed. At least that's what I heard."

Olivia's mouth drops. "Wow! They go to our church. They've always seemed like the perfect family."

"Just goes to show you that perfect isn't always perfect. You don't always know what goes on behind closed doors. At least that's what my mom always says."

CHAPTER 22

Olivia waits for Emma outside the front cafeteria door. Lucky for them, they ended up with the same lunch period.

Emma spots Olivia from down the hall and rushes to her. She whispers: He smiled at me.

Olivia looks around. "Who?"

"That hot guy with the great teeth in my earth science class."

"Oh, the one who knows his rocks."

"Yeah, him. We were passing around a piece of marble and I had to hand it to him. When I did..." she smiles "...our hands touched."

"He's a sophomore, right?"

"Yeah."

"So why's he in earth science and not bio?"

"He took bio last year so that's why he's taking earth science this year," Emma explains.

"That's backward."

"Whatever. Can't you just be happy that he touched me?"

"I'm happy. I'm happy. I'm also hungry."

Olivia and Emma go to the à la carte line and pick up ham and cheese sandwiches and fruit salads.

On their way to a table, several of the girls on Emma's cheerleading squad wave her over.

A tall girl with big silver hoop earrings moves over. "Sit here, Emma. We cheerleaders stick together – on and off the field."

Emma looks at Olivia, then back at the girls. "That's OK. I'm sitting with Libby."

"But she's not one of us," says the petite girl whose breasts are so big you'd think she'd have trouble staying upright.

"It's OK," Olivia whispers to Emma. "If you want to sit with them."

Emma whispers back, "No. I'm sitting with you."

Emma looks at her teammates. "Maybe another time." She follows Olivia to a table on the other side of the cafeteria.

* * *

After Rachel moved, I ate lunch alone. My only companion was whatever book I was reading. Mostly they were romances that I picked up at the used bookstore really cheap. I'd read the books and imagine I was the heroine. The lives I read about in books always seemed to be better than my life. At least the girl always seemed to have someone who loved her. Me? There was Gram and that was it. Not that I wasn't grateful for Gram's love, but it wasn't the same as a boy's.

One day, a guy I had never seen before approached my lunch table. He was blistering hot. He had dark eyes and dark hair that fell to his shoulders. He wore a gray T-shirt that was tight around his bulging biceps. A barbed-wire tattoo wrapped his left arm.

"Mind if I sit here?" he asked.

"Help yourself. There's plenty of room. It's not like there's a crowd fighting to sit with me."

I returned to reading my book and flipped the page.

"That book good?"

"Yeah."

"I'm Chase, by the way. Just moved here."

"Hi. I'm Sarah. Where'd you move from?"

"California."

"So what made you come to the east coast?"

"My dad's job."

Just then Tracey Carmichael and one of her minions strutted over, swinging their hips and sticking out their chests.

"Hi, Chase," said Tracey, throwing back her long black silky hair. "Why don't you sit at our table? You'll be more, uh—" she glared at me and then smiled at him "—comfortable there."

Chase looked at me. "Mind if I move? Since you're reading your book and all."

"Suit yourself."

Chase picked up his tray and followed Tracey to her table where the girls slid down the bench to make room for him. I should have known that Tracey would have her claws into a guy so smokin' hot. Well, at least I had the guys in my books. Fiction for me was definitely better than real life.

*   *   *

"I haven't seen much of Emma lately," Elizabeth tells Olivia. They're on their way to Olivia's dance class.

"Me neither. We're both always busy. I'm usually at dance and now that she's on the cheerleading squad she's either at practice or at games."

"Still, you used to see her more. Is everything all right?"

"Yeah. Everything's great. We're supposed to go to the movies Saturday."

It hasn't been great. Ever since the cafeteria incident, the girls on Emma's squad have tried to alienate Olivia, pulling Emma away every chance they get. Olivia might be at the top of the school food chain, but she's not a cheerleader so it doesn't count.

Olivia's phone rings.

"This is Emma now."

Olivia answers the phone.

"Yeah. (pause) OK. (pause) No, I'm not mad. (double pause) Go to the party. We can go to the movies another time. (pause) I'm sure.(pause) OK. Bye."

"What was that all about?" Elizabeth asks.

"Emma got invited to a party Saturday and wants to go to the party instead of to the movies with me."

"Who's having the party? Can't you go, too?"

"Are you kidding, Mom? One of the cheerleaders is having the party and only cheerleaders are allowed to go. Well, cheerleaders and football players. No one else."

"I see," Elizabeth says. "And how do you feel about that?"

"How do you think I feel? Crummy. My best friend just ditched me to hang with her cheerleader friends. So, yeah, Mom. I don't feel so great. Everything in Emma's life revolves around cheerleading. There's no room for me anymore."

Elizabeth pulls into the parking lot. "Sorry you're going through this, Lib. I hate to see you hurting. I wish I could make it all better."

"Well, you can't, Mom. I'm not a little girl anymore. You just can't kiss my boo-boos and make them all better."

"You're at dance now. Try not to think about it. Concentrate on what you love most of all."

Olivia grabs her dance bag from the back seat, opens the door and gets out. "See you in a couple hours, Mom. And don't worry. I never let anything get in the way of dance. I'd die before I let that happen."

* * *

Chase never sat at my lunch table again. It wasn't long after he started sitting at Tracey's table that they became an item. One day, Chase stopped to talk to me in the hallway. It was just small talk. I think he asked me what book I was reading. Tracey came around the corner and saw us.

She threw back her long black mane and strutted up to us and kissed Chase, taking a little longer than usual for added emphasis. She gave me the death stare, and I knew she would get me back somehow, some day.

It ended up being that day.

I hated gym class. I was the most uncoordinated girl in the entire ninth grade. I couldn't dribble a basketball, hit a softball, kick a soccer ball or get anywhere close to being graceful on the balance beam or uneven bars.

Our gym teacher, Mrs. Montgomery, a middle-aged round woman whose claim to fame was that she won the county tennis championship thirty years ago, made us take showers. She'd herd us into that blue and while tile shower lined with showerheads and we'd get sprinkled and run back out.

I was embarrassed by my body. My right breast was noticeably larger than my left and I always felt the girls' stares and heard their giggles.

When I dashed out of the shower that day, my stuff was gone. I was naked. Dripping wet with no towel, no clothes, no backpack, nothing.

Tracey's locker was a few feet down from mine. She wiggled on her designer jeans. "Missing something?" She laughed.

I covered my privates with my arms and hands the best I could and flashed the meanest look I could muster. My nose flared and my eyes narrowed in on her blemish-free face.

"Look, girls," Tracey said. "Little Miss Goodwill can't dry off or get dressed. Her stuff is missing."

"Where'd you put it, you bitch?"

"Me?" She pulls her silk shirt over her black-widow-spider head. "You couldn't pay me to touch your icky, stinky, second-hand clothes."

The other girls laughed.

The bell rang and they left, laughing, and I was stuck naked in the locker room. I sat down and cried.

"Is someone in here?" Mrs. Montgomery called.

I buried my mouth into my upper arm to muffle my noise. I heard her walk down the center aisle of the locker room. She apparently turned around because the next thing I knew the lights went off and I was alone, huddled in the corner. Naked.

CHAPTER 23

"So are you going to the homecoming?" Lexie asks Olivia on the bus ride home.

Lexie is Olivia's neighbor. She's a year older. She moved into the ivy-covered stone home down the street. The one with the circular driveway and the three-tier granite fountain with scallop edges in the front.

"Mom asked me the same thing this morning," Olivia says. "No one's asked me yet."

"Me neither. But at my old school, you didn't have to be asked. Last year, I went with a bunch of girls. I mean, who needs guys to have a good time, right?"

"Did you have a good time?"

"Totally. My dad rented us a limo. It was the coolest limo I had ever been in. Actually, it was more like a bus that had been totally tricked out. Black leather lounges and chairs and a huge flat screen on the wall. Dad had it stocked with soda and snacks. The driver drove around for an hour and then we had dinner at the country club before going to the dance. After the dance, the limo driver picked us up and Dad had him stop for ice-cream sundaes on the way home. It was so much fun."

"I've never been in a limo before."

"Well, it's way fun. I'm sure my dad would rent a limo for us if I asked him. We could go together. Anyone else you'd want to ask? What about your friend Emma?"

"I heard that she's going with one of the football players."

"I didn't realize you two weren't talking," Lexie said. "I mean, I knew things weren't great, but I didn't know it had gotten to that point."

Olivia had filled Lexie in on the entire saga soon after they met. She liked Lexie. They had a lot in common, including that they were both adopted. Lexie was born in China, though.

"We don't have much to talk about anymore," Olivia says. "All she wants to talk about are the girls on her cheerleading squad and the guys on the football team. She's changed. Or maybe I have."

The bus turns into their street, lined with towering maple trees. They go about two blocks until the bus puts on its flashing yellow then red lights and stops. A red stop sign swings out from the side.

Olivia follows Lexie off the bus. They walk in front of the bus, pausing to look both ways in case an idiot decides to ignore the flashing red lights and stop sign. It happened the other week at a stop across town and a kindergartner was injured. Luckily the bus driver got the license-plate number and they caught the jerk.

When Olivia and Lexie get to the other side, the bus retracts its stop sign, turns off the lights and pulls away.

"So, are you going to think about it?" Lexie asks.

"Sure," Olivia says. "Maybe I'll say something to Mom tonight on our way to dance. See what she thinks."

* * *

I never went to a homecoming dance. No guy ever asked me and, at my school, if you weren't asked by a guy, you didn't go. The idea of a bunch of girls — or guys — going as a group was a more recent development in the history of high school homecomings. Besides, I wouldn't have had anything to wear. And I certainly could never ask Grandma to buy me a fancy dress for just one night. And the costs didn't stop there. Even if you did your own hair and nails and didn't tan or buy the photo package, you still had to pay for the ticket and flowers. That alone was more than we could afford.

Tracey Carmichael had to rub it in that she and Chase were going to the homecoming. Her dad did the whole limo thing, too. Only hers was going to be a white stretch limousine with a fiber-optic starlight. I knew this because she made it a point one day to stop and tell me as she and Chase were walking by. I'm sure she waited until Chase was with her.

Tracey stopped in front of my locker as I was bent over getting the books I needed. "What color's your dress?"

I stood up and turned around. "Excuse me?"

"Your homecoming dress. What color is it?"

"I'm not going."

"Why not?"

I knew that Tracey knew the answer to that question and the only reason she asked it was because she wanted to embarrass me in front of Chase.

"I have something else that night," I lied.

"Glad to hear it's not because you don't have a date," Chase said. "Because I'm sure there are a ton of guys who would love to take you."

Tracey jabbed Chase in his side with her boney elbow. "What's that supposed to mean?" She emphasized the "that".

"I'm just sayin' that Sarah's a pretty girl and there are probably lots of guys who would take her," Chase explained.

Uh-oh. I was in trouble again. Chase said that word "pretty". I knew that he was only trying to be polite, but Tracey was going to make me pay – again.

* * *

"What do you think of going to homecoming with a group of girls?" Olivia asks Elizabeth while driving to dance. Now that Olivia trains at the most prestigious dance academy in the state, there's always plenty of time to talk on the hour drive there and back.

"Sounds fun to me," Elizabeth says. "A daughter of a lady who works for me did that. She said they had more fun than if they had gone with boys they barely knew. Apparently guys go in groups, too. So who would you go with? Emma?"

"Emma has a date. She's going with a football player. He's a junior."

"Really?" Elizabeth says. "I'm surprised her parents let her date someone so much older."

"Not everyone is as protective and as strict as you, Mom."

"I don't think your dad and I are too strict. We just don't see that you need to go out with an older guy. There are plenty of boys your own age."

"You can have sex with a younger guy just as easily as you can have sex with an older one."

Elizabeth coughs. "Lib, I didn't say anything about having sex."

"You didn't have to. I know what you were thinking. Besides, you don't have to worry, Mom. I'm not going to have sex for a long time."

"A long, long time, I hope," Elizabeth says. "But now that you brought it up, I have been wanting to talk to you about some things."

"I know all about the birds and the bees, Mom."

"I'm sure you do. But I want you to know that when you think you're ready for that kind of relationship. When you think you're mature enough to handle that kind of relationship and the emotional baggage that comes with it. Please, for the love of God, talk to me. I will put you on birth control. You know that I don't want you to have sex before you're married, but I'm also not naïve. I know how teenage hormones are. So if you ever get to that point, talk to me. OK?"

"Yes, Mom. I promise to talk to you if and when I decide to have sex. But I really do think that I can probably take care of that myself. The birth control, I mean."

"Sometimes, Lib, things happen fast. So fast that you can't remember how it began. Just be careful."

Olivia is saved from further discussion when they arrive at the dance studio.

"Remember, Dad's picking you up tonight. I need to go back for a meeting. Have a good practice."

"Thanks, Mom. I love you."

"Love you, too."

* * *

I never had anything I loved doing as much as Olivia loves dancing. Grandma taught me how to sew and had hoped that I would love it as much as she did. But, it wasn't for me. I could sew simple things, like window valances or pillow covers, but that was about it.

Most times I put puzzles together. Grandma brought them home from yard sales or the Goodwill store. If I was really lucky, which was almost never, all of the pieces would be there.

I remember the puzzle I was working on when I got that first prank call from Tracey. It was a fall landscape with lots of reds and yellows and oranges. I had completed the border and was working on the farmhouse. The phone rang and Grandma wasn't home so I let it go into voicemail. I didn't feel like talking.

After the phone rang a few times, the answering machine clicked on.

"Hello," Grandma said. "You've reached the home of Grace and Sarah. We aren't home at the moment, but if you leave your name and number we'll return your call."

"Sarah,' the voice said.

I stopped searching for the chimney piece and listened.

"I was just calling to see if you got the results back from your pregnancy test. I'm worried about you."

Then the phone clicked.

It wasn't Tracey's voice, but I was sure she was behind it. If Grandma would have heard it, I would have had some explaining to do. Mostly why someone would hate me so much to leave a message like that. But it was just the beginning of the prank calls. They would continue over the next two years. Some I would catch before Grandma heard them and some I wouldn't. It was always the ones that I didn't get to before Grandma that seemed to be the worst.

* * *

"Hey, Lib," Lexie says as she approaches the bus stop. "Think about homecoming last night?"

"Yeah. I'll go."

"Great. Already talked to Dad and he said he'll get us a limo. Who else should we ask?"

"Don't you have anyone you know from your classes?" Olivia says.

"Not really. The girls haven't been real friendly here. Except you, of course."

"They probably view you as competition."

"Me, competition?"

"Absolutely. Have you looked in the mirror lately? You are a model, after all."

"You promised not to tell anyone," Lexie says. "I don't want anyone to know that part of my life. It makes them see me differently."

"Yeah. You're even more of a threat," Olivia says. "But your secret's safe with me."

"You know I only model because it's something fun to do. It's really no big deal."

"I know it's no big deal to you, but, to the girls at the top of the food chain, they would kill to have their picture plastered all over glossy magazines and catalogs."

"I'm getting out of that anyway," Lexie says.

"Why?"

"Getting tired of it. I want a break. I figure moving here gives me a chance to be a regular girl at a regular school where no one knows anything about any of that stuff."

Olivia laughs. "I don't think you'll ever be regular, but you're definitely the coolest girl I know. Mostly because you don't know how cool you are or care. You're just you."

The girls talk about homecoming the entire bus ride to school. What, if any, girls to invite along in the limo? Where to shop for a dress? Should they tan, get manicures and pedicures? By the time the bus pulls up to the school, Olivia is actually excited about something other than dance. I haven't see her this happy in quite some time, and it fills me with warmth.

Olivia turns the corner to go to her locker and sees Emma waiting for her.

"Hi," says Emma as Olivia pulls her backpack off her right shoulder.

"Hi."

"I miss you."

"Oh, really. You could have fooled me. You seem to be enjoying hanging with your new friends."

"They're not like you. I only pretend to like them so much to fit in."

"You shouldn't have to pretend," Olivia says. "It takes more courage to be you, even if that means standing alone, than to be part of a crowd. And besides, a friend doesn't treat a friend the way you've treated me, ditching me for them and canceling our plans."

Just then a group of cheerleaders see Emma and run up to her.

"Emma," says the tall girl with the hourglass body and endless legs. "I just asked the girls who they thought was the most popular girl in our grade. They said me."

The girls giggle.

"What do you think?"

"Definitely," Emma says.

Endless Legs laughs. "I just love you all."

Emma looks at Olivia and mouths sorry and then turns to go with her friends.

Olivia is stunned. It's true. The girl probably is the most popular girl in the entire ninth grade. But she knows it. She just asked the others so she could hear them say it and feel good about herself. A real piece of work, Olivia thinks.

* * *

Tracey was a real piece of work, too. When I confronted her about the prank phone call, she snickered.

"That's so funny," she said. "Leaving a message about getting pregnancy test results. I'll have to remember that one."

"I know it was you, Tracey. Well, not you, you. But someone you put up to it."

"Tsk. Tsk. Tsk," Tracey said. "Shouldn't accuse someone of something you can't prove. Are you hungry?"

"What?"

"I just wondered if you and your grandma need some food. I see the cans for the food bank are piling up in the lobby. I'm sure school officials won't mind if you take some cans from the food drive home so you and Grandma dearest can eat. Since you get food from there, it would save you a trip."

I hung my head and walked away. I hated that Tracey always had the last word, and it usually cut the deepest.

CHAPTER 24

The super stretch black Town Car limo pulls up to Lexie's house where Tom and Elizabeth have joined Lexie's parents to take pictures of the girls.

"Now, let's get one of you and your mom and dad," says Lexie's mom, Lila.

I've never seen so many photos taken at one time. There's Lexie and Lila. Lexie and her dad. Lexie and her mom and dad. Lexie alone. Lexie and Olivia. Olivia alone. Olivia with her mom and dad. Olivia with her mom. Olivia with her dad.

"We forgot about Daisy," Olivia says.

Daisy's lying under the nearby sycamore tree. Her ears perk up when she hears her name. She barks and runs to Olivia. Olivia picks her up and puts her face next to Daisy's. Elizabeth snaps the photo.

"Anything else anyone wants to take a picture of?" Lila asks.

"Get us getting into the limo," Lexie says.

More photos are taken.

"Now, remember. Get what you want to eat at the club," Lexie's dad says. "I've called ahead and they're expecting you."

"Thanks, Dad."

Lexie hugs her parents and Olivia hugs hers.

The limo driver holds the door open and the girls climb in. Black leather seating wraps around forming a "J". There's a mirrored ceiling with neon lighting and a cherry-wood bar stocked with fresh ice and the diet soda and water the girls have requested.

The parents wave as the limo pulls away and Lexie and Olivia turn on the stereo and the flat screen and pour drinks using the beautiful crystal glasses in the console.

* * *

I can't imagine the cost of such indulgence. I have nothing to compare it to, and yet I'm happy that Olivia is happy and that she has Lexie as a friend.

After Rachel moved, we lost touch. Not right away, but over time. Sort of how a beautiful beach changes and erodes. The beach vanishes altogether if no one does anything to stop it.

I remember Rachel telling me about the time she went to the beach on a family vacation and how stunned she was to see that it was half the size it had been the year before. She said she watched workers dredge sand from way out in the ocean and deposit it along the vanishing beach. I wish I would have dredged in our friendship. You just don't always know the most significant pieces of your life until they're gone and it's too late to get them back. There were so many times I could have picked up the phone and didn't.

"How's Rachel?" Tracey asked me one day in the locker room.

"What do you care? You never liked her."

"True. Although I thought she had more potential than you."

The other girls laughed.

"You know, Tracey," I said. "You're really lucky to have a pretty face."

Tracey looked at me as if she had just won Publishers Clearing House.

"Because you sure don't have anything else going for you." I clicked my padlock shut and spun the dial.

"Bitch. I'll get you back for that, you fat slut."

I'll never forget how good that felt. I knew I pissed Tracey off and that things would probably get worse. But I tried to enjoy the moment, knowing that it, like the beautiful beach, wouldn't last forever.

* * *

"Did you hear?" Lexie asks Olivia during the limo ride to the club for dinner.

"About what?"

"About Mr. Miller."

"What about Miller?"

"He's gone."

Lexie refills her glass with more Diet Pepsi and adds a lemon slice.

"But I just saw him yesterday in Art," Olivia says.

"I doubt you'll see him again. He supposedly was doing one of his students."

"Oh! My! Gawd! Which one?"

"Don't know. But I heard she turned him in when he stopped paying her."

Olivia's eyes bugged out. "He was paying her for sex?"

"And bojos, or so I've heard."

"Bojos?"

"Blow jobs, dummy. You do know what they are?"

Olivia nods.

"Did you ever do that?" Lexie asks.

"What?"

"A bojo."

Olivia coughs and spits out the water she just sipped all over her strapless fuchsia dress.

Lexie reaches for the box of tissues sitting on the console on her right. "Sorry. Didn't mean to make you cough."

"I've only ever kissed a boy," Olivia says. "It's not like I wouldn't want to do more, well, maybe not a bojo, but there's no guy I've ever been that interested in. What about you?"

"I've definitely made out with a few guys. Not the whole way, but pretty close."

"Weren't you scared?"

"A little. But I'd been reading my mom's steamy romance novels like forever. I knew kind of where to touch and kiss. Never got to third base though."

I know what Olivia's thinking and her innocence warms me. I was a lot like her when I was her age. Not too bright in the making-out department – mostly from a lack of experience. But I didn't have a Lexie to educate me.

She finally gets up enough courage to ask. "What exactly are the bases anyway?"

"You seriously don't know?"

Olivia shakes her head. "Sort of, but…"

"It's OK. I didn't know until someone explained it to me. She was older, too. Here's the deal. First base is French kissing. Second base is above the waist, like letting the guy feel up under your shirt. Third is below the waist. Like letting the guy finger you or giving bojos. The last base is home, which is going all the way."

Olivia takes a deep breath. "Got it. And you got to second base?"

"Yeah. Lots of times. Never to third. There was this girl at my old school, though, who cut out the crotch in her underwear so her boyfriend could finger her in class or at lunch. They were always on third base."

"That's disgusting."

"Yeah, tell me about it. She bragged about it all the time. Funny thing happened though. She was wearing a pair of her homemade crotchless panties and forgot to put spankies on under her cheerleading skirt."

"Uh-oh," Olivia says.

"Yeah. Uh-oh. She did a flip and flashed everyone and it's all anyone talked about for weeks. They called her Cat after that."

"Cat?"

"P-u-s-..."

Olivia wrinkles her nose. "I get it. I get it."

"She's the same girl who had an oral-sex party in eighth grade and invited four couples. Well, one guy had two girls because one guy had to leave early."

"Two girls at once?"

"Apparently."

"So they all came to her house for oral sex?"

"Yeah. She lived with her dad, who was never home. They gathered in her bedroom, which someone told me was really small, and made out at the same time."

"In front of each other!"

"Guess the lights were out."

"Still. That's disgusting."

* * *

One thing I love about being Olivia's moment keeper is the normal teenage moments I get to experience through her. I never had these kinds of conversations with a girlfriend and while it's kind of scary to know she's thinking about all of this stuff, it also seems so natural and normal. Young girls are supposed to have these types of conversations. It's part of growing up. I think I was the abnormal one. In fact, Tracey had convinced the entire school I was the abnormal one.

After my comment in the locker room, she turned up the dial a couple notches. And this time, she got a guy involved.

For days, I felt his dark eyes on me as I walked to my locker. His locker was across from mine and he'd stand there and watch me. He was definitely hot, too hot to be looking at me, I thought. But the more he watched me, the more I began to think that maybe, just maybe, he thought I was pretty. He even started to smile.

Finally, I got up enough nerve to say something to him. I closed my locker and walked over as he was closing his locker. "Where's your class?"

He nodded. "Down the hall."

"Want to walk together?"

A Grinch-like smirk erupted on his face. "If I wanted to ask an ugly bitch like you to walk to class, I would have asked you."

I was horrified. I couldn't move. And then I heard Tracey. As I stood there trembling, trying to hold back the searing tears that pooled in my eyes, Tracey kissed Dark Eyes on the cheek and handed him a fifty-dollar bill. "Well done, Romeo." Then she looked at me. "Seriously, Sarah. Do you really think anyone would actually be interested in the Goodwill Poster Child?"

And she laughed and so did everyone else.

I couldn't believe it. I had made a complete ass out of myself. All that time I thought he was interested in me and he wasn't. He was just pretending to be to make a quick fifty from Tracey. She paid him just to toy with me and lure me into his web so she could sink her fangs into me. I didn't realize Tracey and her minions had been watching, waiting. Guess she knew, or hoped, that I would eventually work up enough nerve to approach Dark Eyes. She might not have known what I would say or what he would say, but she was paying him enough to hit as hard as he could when he had the chance. And stupid I gave him just that.

* * *

The limo driver pulls up to the school and a crowd of teens in suits and gowns of varying styles and colors gathers to gawk. Olivia and Lexie step out of the stretch and there are whistles from the crowd. The girls look stunning – Olivia in her strapless fuchsia dress and Lexie in the black silk number she fell in love with during a model shoot for a teen magazine earlier in the year. She told Olivia she bought the dress hoping she'd have a chance to wear it.

Olivia and Lexie find a table with some other girls who came as a group.

"Mind if we join you?" Olivia asks.

"You want to sit here? With us?" says a short, chunky girl with thick glasses and short red hair.

"Of course. Why wouldn't we?" Olivia says.

Lexie agrees. "You're nice. Right? You don't bite or anything."

The chunky girl smiles. "I'm Delaney and this is Molly and Jackie. We're in ninth grade."

"I'm Olivia."

"I know who you are," Delaney says. "I've see you dance before and you're amazing."

"Thanks," Olivia says. "And this is my friend Lexie."

"You look so familiar," Molly says. "But I don't think we've ever met. Oh. I know. I know. You look like a model in one of my magazines. Doesn't she, girls?"

Delaney and Jackie turn toward Lexie and shrug their shoulders.

"I totally see it," Molly says. "I'm going to have to dig that magazine out and show you."

"That's OK," Lexie says. "I've heard of people having doubles. Guess the model's mine."

Emma and her date walk off the dance floor and Emma sees Olivia sitting at the table. She walks over. "Nice dress, Lib."

"Thanks. Yours, too. You look good in yellow."

"Are you going to dance?" Emma asks.

"Maybe later."

"I keep telling her to get out on the dance floor but she keeps dragging her feet," Lexie says.

"Well, see ya later," Emma says and walks away.

"I hate those cheerleaders," Delaney says. "They make fun of me. One time there was a picture of Miss Piggy on my locker and I know one of them put it there."

"That's awful," Lexie says. "Just ignore them. Might even try smiling at them. Make them think you know something they don't. It'll bug the shit out of them."

Delaney laughs. "I like you, Lexie. You're prettier than any of them and you don't act like a jerk. You, too, Olivia."

"That's because Lib and I aren't out to impress people. If you like us, great. If you don't, your loss."

Olivia agrees. "People who try to be someone special never are."

* * *

I wish I would have had a Lexie or Olivia in my life. I wish Rachel hadn't moved. Maybe it would have made a difference. If I would have had someone, besides Grandma, who made me feel like I mattered, who actually loved me. But when you live your whole life being treated like dirt – people walk on you and spit on you and kick you – it's hard to see yourself as anything else. Hell, I wasn't even good soil. I was the severely compacted kind that nothing could ever grow in.

I remember my science fair experiment in elementary school. I planted seeds in three different types of soil to determine which soil was best. The day I was to present my project to the class, I had to take it on the bus with me because Grandma couldn't drive me to school. I was so careful. I didn't want anyone bumping into it or messing it up. Unfortunately, when I got off the bus, Tracey and her minions were nearby.

"What's that?" asked Tracey, cracking bubbles in her mouth.

"It's her science fair project," a Tracey clone said.

Tracey pushed the girl into me. I lost my balance and struggled to keep from falling.

Tracey and her friends laughed and walked away. I managed to get my science experiment to the classroom without any more trouble. The best part? I got an "A", and that was something that even Tracey, who seemed to wield more power than anyone I knew, couldn't take away from me.

* * *

I watch as Olivia, Lexie and the girls at their table head to the dance floor. It's crowded but they find a sliver of space toward the back.

Olivia and Lexie pick up the beat and their bodies contort and move in ways that amaze me. Delaney, Molly and Jackie aren't moving too much. They notice that people are stopping to watch Olivia. Lexie is still dancing, but it's Olivia who's taking over the dance floor.

"Loosen up," Olivia tells Delaney, Molly and Jackie. "Feel the beat. Close your eyes if you want to. Just let your body respond to the music."

"You da shizzle," says Lexie, trying to copy some of Olivia's moves.

More and more people stop to watch Olivia and pretty soon Lexie and the girls stop to watch, too. Olivia is oblivious to what's happening around her. She's completely in the zone and it isn't until the music stops and people clap that she realizes they have been watching her.

"You're amazing," Delaney says. "I wish I could dance like that."

"Thanks," Olivia says. "And you can if you want to. I could teach you."

"You'd really do that for me?" Delaney asks.

"Sure. For all of you. We can meet once a week or something. How about you, Lex?"

"I'm totally in. It'll be fun."

"I always wanted to teach dance and have my own studio," Olivia says. "This will give me a chance to see if I like the teaching part."

The girls are inseparable the rest of the night. And when the limo driver comes to pick up Olivia and Lexie, the three others get into the car, too, calling their parents ahead of time to make sure it's OK.

CHAPTER 25

Olivia stands in the hallway talking to Delaney when a girl taps her on the shoulder.

"Special delivery."

"For me?"

"Yep."

The girl hands Olivia several white carnations, a couple pink and several red. The student council sold carnations for Valentine's Day and student representatives are delivering them.

"Wow. You got a lot of admirers," Delaney says.

Olivia holds the bundle up to her nose and sniffs. "Want some?"

Delaney shakes her head. "I'm not going to take your flowers, Lib."

"You're not taking them; I'm giving them to you."

"Same thing."

"Is not. Well, at least take a red one. It'll keep the piranhas guessing."

Olivia hands Delaney a red carnation and Delaney's slight smile slides into a showing-teeth grin.

* * *

I got a red carnation once. It was a long time ago. I think I was in ninth grade, too. Like Olivia's school, the carnations were sold as a Valentine's Day fundraiser. Never did find out who sent me the flower, but I remember that when Tracey saw me in the hallway with it she snickered.

"Someone actually sent you a red carnation?" she said.

She emphasized "you". As in *I can't believe anyone in their right mind would ever send you a red carnation because you're so obviously worthless and ugly and you so don't matter.*

But someone did and I kept that carnation forever. I pressed it and put it in the black Bible embossed with my name in gold that Grandma had given me for confirmation. I can still picture the red carnation, tucked into the Bible at first Corinthians, chapter thirteen, verse thirteen. "And now these three remain: faith, hope and love. But the greatest of these is love."

The day I got the flower, I kept looking around to see if there was a nod, some sort of sign or recognition from the guy who sent it. But there was nothing. So I spent time picturing him in my mind, conjuring up an image that fit the knight in shining armor I hoped one day would whisk me away to his castle.

He was tall and strong with black hair. And piercing dark eyes that cradled me in a sweet stillness and made me feel as if I was the most important person in the world. An easy smile that exuded warmth and made my body tingle with desire. Muscular arms that wrapped around me and kept me safe, always safe from the cruel Traceys of the world.

That was my dream. My forever dream. I guess some dreams, no matter how much we want them and pray for them, aren't meant to be.

* * *

Olivia gives all her carnations away. She feels so good giving one to Delaney that she decides to give them to others who are flowerless. She figures they would enjoy them more than she does. So she walks down the hall, handing flowers to girls and guys until they're gone.

As she heads to class she runs into some cheerleaders in a huddle near the doors to the gym. Their arms are overflowing with carnations, most of them red. They turn to look at Olivia.

"I would have thought you'd have at least one carnation," Most Popular Girl in the Ninth Grade says.

Olivia shrugs her shoulders. "Sorry to disappoint you."

"Well, we can't all be popular. There has to be regular girls, too."

"Yep, I'm a regular girl."

Olivia can't help but smile once she passes them. She hates that they always make it a competition to see who gets the most carnations. She figures they probably buy them or bring extra to school — hiding them in their backpacks — on distribution day to make sure they have more than anyone else.

"Hey, Lib," Lexie calls.

Olivia turns to see Lexie with a dozen red carnations. "Looks like someone likes you a lot."

"Yeah, it's Tallen. He couldn't keep it a secret."

Lexie has been dating Tallen for a month, and she likes him a lot. He's a senior.

"Can you come over to practice dance tomorrow?"

"If we do it in the afternoon. Tallen's taking me to the movies tomorrow night."

Ever since the dance, Delaney, Molly and Jackie have been hanging with Lexie and Olivia. Olivia kept her promise about teaching them to dance. When she has time, which is rarely ever, they practice at her house.

"Tallen's best friend, Cole, goes to Catholic High," Lexie says. "He wondered if you liked to double date sometime."

"Maybe, let me think about it."

"He's cute. I saw pictures of him."

"I'll think about it. Promise."

"Oh, almost forgot," Lexie says. "Mom and Dad are going away next weekend. I'm thinking about having a small party. I could invite Cole."

"We'll talk later," Olivia says. "Gotta get to class."

Olivia walks into history class and sees Emma. Emma wipes her blotchy face with a tissue.

"Everything all right?" Olivia asks.

"Justin broke up with me."

"Today?"

"Last night. Then I got all these stupid carnations today. Since the orders were placed weeks ago, they're probably from him."

"Sorry, Em," Olivia says. "I know you liked him a lot."

Mr. Tuttle walks in. "Get out your books and turn to page two hundred and fifty."

* * *

The minute I heard Lexie mention "parents away" and "party" I got worried. I know what can happen when teens party. They drink too much and do stupid things they would never do if it were not for the influence of alcohol.

I know from personal experience. When I was sixteen, I met this guy at the grocery store where I worked. I ran a cash register and he stocked shelves.

Travis was older than me and went to a different school. He was the first guy who ever paid any kind of attention to me. Could have been because he was so obviously gay, but I didn't care. He was my friend, and I hadn't had one of those in a long time.

One night, Travis and his friends got a couple cases of beer and invited me to go with them to an abandoned cabin in the woods. The only alcohol I had up until that point was Communion wine. The beers went down fast. Too fast.

"Are you OK?" Travis asked me.

I had managed to make it away from the campfire to a big oak tree beside the cabin. I leaned against the tree and threw up.

"I'll be OK."

"Sure?"

"Yeah. Just give me a minute."

Travis helped me to his car and took me home. Grandma was waiting up for me and was she spitting bullets.

"Look at you. Drunk as a skunk. Just like your dad. I thought you had better sense than that!"

"Don't ever say I'm like my dad."

"Well, then don't act like him."

I could taste the vomit in my throat and feel it working its way up. I dashed to the toilet but didn't make it in time. I barfed all over the bathroom floor. I had never been so sick, and I knew that I never wanted to feel that way again.

When I woke up the next morning, I didn't even know how I got to bed. The last thing I remember was throwing up in the bathroom and crashing on the floor. I had the worst headache of my life.

I was moaning when Grandma walked in.

"How do you feel this morning?"

"Terrible. My head's pounding."

"Serves you right for doing something so dumb."

"Sorry, Gram."

"Don't sorry me. I'm really disappointed in you, Sarah. Thought you had more smarts than that."

"I never had alcohol before, Gram. I swear."

"Well, if you know what's good for you, you won't drink like that again."

Grandma took care of me that day, but she never let me forget how drunk I was. And whenever she'd compare the state I was in that night to Matt's frequent binges, it was enough to make me swear off alcohol forever. Plus, I just didn't feel as if getting drunk was worth feeling so lousy the next day.

So, yeah, hearing Lexie talk about having a party makes me nervous for Olivia. I'd hate to see her get drunk and feel like crap the next day. I wish moment keepers could stop moments from happening. But we can't. It's our job to simply observe and record.

I now know how a parent must feel about their child. It's like you want your kids to make good decisions and do the right things, but you know that they aren't always going to. And when they don't, you hurt for them. You understand that it's a part of growing up, of maturing. But that doesn't make it any easier. Especially when you see there's going to be a train wreck and you can't do a damn thing to prevent it. This, perhaps, is the hardest part of being a moment keeper. The times when I know what's coming and wish I could stop it but I can't. I'm helpless. I can't battle free will.

* * *

Lexie's mom, Lila, peeks in Lexie's door. "Are you sure you're going to be OK for the weekend?"

"I'll be fine, Mom. Lib's spending the night."

"Yeah, Mrs. Russo. I'll watch out for her."

"OK. But you have all of the phone numbers — the cell-phone numbers, the main number of the hotel where we're staying, the direct line to the room."

"Mom, I'll be fine. Just go and enjoy yourselves. I'm sixteen now."

"And if she needs anything, my parents are right around the corner."

As soon as they hear the garage door go down and Lexie's parents drive away from the house, the girls turn up the music and dance around shouting, "Par-TY! Par-TY! Par-TY!"

"So what's the plan?" Olivia asks.

"Tallen and a few of his friends should be here around seven. Molly, Delaney and Jackie are coming at six so we have two hours to get things ready. Want a drink?"

"Of what?"

"Let's check Dad's bar. See what's there."

Olivia follows Lexie to the lower level. An L-shaped cherry bar with eight stools sits in one corner. A black leather sectional surrounds a seventy-two-inch flat screen in another corner.

Olivia notices the poker table. "Looks like it's set to play."

"Yeah. Dad keeps it that way. He got a new pinball machine. Want to see it?"

Olivia follows Lexie into the adjacent game room with a pool table, air-hockey table, jukebox and a few pinball machines.

"It's this one." Lexie taps the pinball machine.

The classic machine is white with black and red geometric shapes on the sides. It's titled Outer Space.

"Looks old," Olivia says.

"It is. Dad only buys old machines that have been restored. This is one he played as a kid in some pizza shop he always went to. He looked for that particular machine forever."

Lexie's cell phone rings. "It's Tallen."

"I'll wait in the other room."

"Go ahead and get a drink if you want."

Olivia checks out the bar. She's never seen so many bottles of liquor. They line shelves on the mirrored hutch behind the bar. Gin. Vodka. Crown Royal. Bailey's Irish Cream. Kahlua. Seagram's VO. Bacardi rum, Tequila. Brandy. Cognac. Johnnie Walker Black Scotch. Jim Beam bourbon. Olivia skips the liquor and finds a Diet Pepsi in the refrigerator under the bar next to the built-in in dishwasher and sink.

A few minutes later, Lexie walks in. "So what'd you get?"

"Diet Pepsi for now. Everything OK with Tallen?"

"Yeah. He's picking Cole up at six-thirty. I can't wait for you to meet him."

"Is he bringing anyone else?"

"That's what he called about. Two of his friends are working and won't be over until nine."

Lexie gets a glass, fills it with ice and some gin and diet tonic water. "Mom drinks this but she usually puts a slice of lime in it. Guess a squirt of lime juice will have to do since we're all out of limes."

She gets the lime juice from the refrigerator and pours a little in the glass and stirs it with a plastic stirrer. "Want a taste?"

Olivia shakes her head. "Maybe later."

"Lib." Lexie puts on her serious face. "If you don't see Tallen and me down here, don't freak. We might be in my bedroom."

"OK. I won't freak, but are you sure you're ready for that?"

"At least third base, maybe I'll go for a homerun."

"But you've only been dating a month," Olivia says.

"It's not like I'm a slut, Lib, and going to start sleeping around."

"I didn't mean it like that. What I really meant is for you to make sure you want to give him that. That's all I'm saying. It's yours to give, when you're ready. Not his to take when he's ready."

* * *

Olivia's advice makes me proud. I think her mom would be, too, although she'd be mortified that Olivia was even having such a conversation. I wish I would have had an Olivia to talk some sense into me when I was sixteen. Grandma tried, but by that time she was beginning to get sick and I just don't think she had the energy.

It was the summer before my junior year in high school when I met Bryan. And it was a summer that changed my life forever.

CHAPTER 26

By the time Molly, Delaney and Jackie arrive, Lexie's slurring her words.

"She OK?" Delaney asks Olivia.

"Yeah, she's on her third gin and tonic. Next one I'll make for her."

I can read Olivia's mind and I know that she'll skip the gin and just use tonic water and a splash of lime. She figures Lexie won't know the difference.

"Want a drink?" Lexie asks.

The girls follow her to the bar.

"Coke for me," Delaney says.

"Howsabout a little rum in that Coke?" asks Lexie, thrusting her head from side to side.

"OK. But just a little."

Lexie pours more than just a little but Delaney takes the drink anyway.

"I'll have what she's having," Molly says.

Jackie pulls out a stool and climbs up. "Me, too."

"Rum and Cokes for all my besties," Lexie says.

Olivia walks behind the bar. "Here, let me help you."

"I can do it myselves," Lexie says. "Howsabout getting the music?"

Olivia turns on the music and the girls sit around the bar and swap gossip.

"Did you hear what happened when they had the drug dogs at school the other day?" Jackie asks.

"I heard Josh Blanchard got nailed," Delaney says.

"Yeah. The dogs targeted his car and the cops found pot. The dogs also stopped at JR Dunlap's Jeep. They didn't find drugs but they did find a knife."

"Not smart," Olivia says.

"You got that right," Jackie continues. "It was a box cutter. Apparently it came from the warehouse where he works. He forgot to take it out of his pocket one day and left it in his car. So he might be expelled because he had a weapon on school property."

"A box cutter's a weapon?" Molly asks.

"Hell," Jackie says. "A toenail clipper's a weapon. Remember that first-grader who was expelled for having a small toenail clipper in his backpack? Anyway, JR's parents got a lawyer and are fighting it. They also found over-the-counter cold medicine in Ashley Tanner's car and she got in trouble for that."

"Zero tolerance is so dumb," Olivia says. "Cold medicine. Really? The world isn't black and white. I think you should look at each case individually."

Lexie raises her glass. "I'll drink to that."

The girls raise their glasses and take a swig.

* * *

I have to agree with Olivia. Life isn't black and white. The black blurs into the white creating gradients. Authority figures don't like gradients. They like to keep things simple. Right or wrong. Black or White. Not sort of right and sort of wrong. Or sort of black and sort of white. It's either one or the other. There's no room for in between.

But they're wrong. Sometimes the right answer is the wrong answer and the wrong answer is the right answer and sometimes they're both a little of each. It's all a matter of perspective. Life is weird like that. We can all look at a painting and see something different. I might see pain and you might see joy. That's how life is. When people looked at my life, they probably thought it was pretty OK. I had a grandmother who adored me. I had it better than some people who had parents! And yet what they didn't see was the loneliness and worthlessness I felt. The times when I was overcome with despair so heavy I could hardly breathe. Having your dad reject you will do that to you.

"Sarah," Grandma said one day. "Why do you always look at the glass half empty?"

"It's not that I always look at it half empty, I'm just realistic," I told her. "No sense in wishing for things that can never be."

"It's not about wishing for the impossible," Grandma said. "It's about having hope that life has some pretty good cards in store for you. Maybe not a royal flush, but it could be a straight or four of a kind. That's still pretty darn good."

"Gram," I said. "I can't play poker. I don't have a poker face. I'll fold my hand every time."

The next day I found an Ace of Hearts on my dresser with a note from Gram. It said: Always keep an Ace in the hole.

* * *

The girls are doing karaoke and the doorbell rings.

"Shhsa," Lexie says. "Hear that?"

Olivia turns off the music. The bell rings again.

"They're here," Lexie says. "Omigod. How do I look? Do I look sexy?"

She turns all pouty lips and twists her head as if she's posing for one of her cameramen at a magazine photo shoot.

"You look great," Olivia says. "Want us to come with you?"

"Nah," Lexie says. "You just get ready to Par-Ty."

When Lexie returns with Tallen and Cole, the girls are sitting at the bar.

Lexie leans on Tallen and they walk over. Cole follows a few steps behind. I know it's a cliché, but he really is tall, dark and handsome. His dark curly hair frames his face and his eyes are so dark they look black. The minute Olivia sees Cole I'm startled by a feeling I've never felt before. Olivia is going to fall head over heels for this guy. I feel it and I know she feels it. Her stomach tingles and she grabs it, caught off guard by the strong attraction she feels for someone she hasn't even been introduced to yet.

Tallen asks Olivia, "How much has Lex had?"

"Three."

"Nosa I didn't. I had four," says Lexie, holding up five fingers.

Olivia winks and Tallen gives a slight nod, enough to acknowledge that he gets what Olivia is trying to say without saying it – the fourth drink was sans alcohol.

"Well, girls. You all know Tallen, my sweets," Lexie says. "This is Cole, his bestie. Cole, this is Jackie and Delaney and Molly and Olivia."

Cole nods to each girl, but when he gets to Olivia his dark eyes are drawn to her green ones as an electron is drawn to a proton. He brushes his five o'clock shadow with the palm of his right hand and flashes teeth so white Olivia is convinced he must bleach them. I think everyone notices the spark and I immediately worry that the winds of time will fan it into an inferno.

"Would you like something to drink?" Olivia asks the guys.

"What's on draft?" Cole asks.

"Blue Moon," Lexie says.

They each want a draft.

Olivia gets two frosty mugs from the freezer and Tallen and Lexie head for the leather sectional.

"Want me to pour?" Cole asks. "There's an art to pouring so you don't get too much head."

Delaney, Molly and Jackie laugh. Olivia gives them her beadiest evil eyes by scrunching them so much they become slits.

Cole takes the frosty mug from Olivia and tilts it under the tap at about a forty-five-degree angle.

"When the glass is about half full, turn it to a ninety-degree angle. You want to pour in the middle of the glass. And you want..." he looks at Delaney, Molly and Jackie "...an inch or so of head on it."

"What's so good about head anyhow?" Molly asks.

Everyone laughs.

"For one thing, it looks good. For another, it releases the beer's aromatics," Cole says.

"It's what?" Molly asks.

"It makes the beer taste better," Olivia says.

Cole looks at Olivia. "Next one you can pour."

"How'd you learn so much about pouring beer?" Olivia asks.

"Watched my dad. He owns a bar."

The girls look over and see Lexie sitting on Tallen's lap. She's rubbing his head and grinding.

"We need to cut her off," Molly says.

"Already done," Olivia tells them.

"So, Cole. Tell us about Catholic High. What's it like?" Delaney asks.

"Like your school, only we have religion classes."

"I'd hate that," Delaney says.

"It's not too bad."

"My parents are always trying to get me to go to church. Just not sure I buy the whole God thing," Delaney says.

"That's it," Olivia says. "No talking religion."

Olivia and Delaney have gotten into this debate before and Olivia really isn't up to having a serious conversation about it now. She's tried to convince Delaney that God is real, that Heaven is real, but Delaney is stubborn. She just can't bring herself to believe in something she can't touch or see or hear.

"Let's dance," Molly says, trying to break the tension. The girls go to an open space near the poker table to dance. Olivia and Cole stay at the bar to talk.

* * *

I feel as if I'm spying on Olivia. I guess I am in a way. I'm recording all of her moments, watching and filing them away to recall later. While we record everything, moment keepers don't share everything at the end. We choose those moments that matter. Maybe it's a moment that shows growth or leads to an understanding of why something is one way and not another. Each moment is carefully picked to play a part in the final showing of each life story. It's like editing a movie and deciding which moments best depict the person's life in a way that leads to acceptance and understanding.

Sometimes, I know immediately that I will include a moment as I'm recording it. I just recognize its significance instantly. I've gotten better at this over the years, too. I know I will include, for example, when Olivia and Cole met for the first time. Something inside of me tells me that they will be connected forever. I'm not sure exactly how yet. I don't see moments ahead of time. It's just something I feel.

* * *

"Tallen says you're a dancer," Cole says.

Olivia sips her Diet Pepsi, which she had added rum to when she refilled her glass. "Yeah. Dancing's pretty much my life. It's what I want to do forever. How about you?"

"I'm thinking about medicine. Maybe bio. Wouldn't mind being a doctor. Just got back my SAT scores and I did unbelievably well. Even my guidance counselor called me down to the office to talk about them. Said that I was a bit of an underachiever in school but the SATs showed my true potential."

"So what's next?" Olivia asks.

"Can't start applying until late summer. I have my top five schools picked and I'll probably throw in a couple of others just to be safe."

"Are you two gonna join us?" Delaney asks Lexie and Tallen. "Or are you just going to make out all night?"

Lexie gets off Tallen, takes his hand and pulls him off the couch. "We're coming."

Olivia and Cole join in, too.

"Wait," Jackie says. "I think I hear something."

Delaney turns down the music. "It's the doorbell again. Isn't it early for the other guys to be here? You said they weren't coming until nine."

Olivia goes upstairs and peeks out the window and runs back downstairs. I notice her left eye and thumb are twitching.

"Crap. It's my mom and dad. Lexie, you'd better come with me. The rest of you must be really, really quiet. They're probably just stopping by to make sure Lexie and I don't need anything."

Olivia and Lexie go upstairs. Olivia pulls out a chair in the kitchen. "Sit here. I'll answer the door. Just yell in that you're making pizza. Got it?"

"I gots it."

Olivia opens the door. "Hi, guys."

"Hey, Lib. We were on our way home and wanted to make sure you and Lexie didn't need anything," Elizabeth says.

"We're fine, Mom. Lexie's in the kitchen making pizza."

"Hi, Mr. and Mrs. Kennedy. I'm making cookies."

"I thought you said she was making pizza?" Olivia's dad asks.

"We're making both."

"Such little Suzy Homemakers," Elizabeth says. "Well, if you need anything we'll be home the rest of the night. Love you."

"Love you too, Mom."

Olivia hugs her parents and says goodbye and walks into the kitchen. "Now that was a close one."

"Thinks sa believed you?" Lexie asks.

"I think so."

The girls return to the basement and give the all-clear signal. Delaney turns on the music and the partying starts again. Olivia follows Cole over to the bar and he pours another draft. "Want to try it?"

"I think I'll stick with the Diet Pepsi and rum," Olivia says. "Do you drink a lot?"

Cole shakes his head. "Been around it all of my life since my dad owns a bar. Never did much for me. I never wanted it to get in the way of baseball. Plus, I've seen lots of drunks who waste their lives sitting on a bar stool downing Jack."

* * *

Matt was one of those drunks so I knew just what Cole was talking about. I can still picture Matt sitting at the bar with some floozy hanging on his arm, slobbering like an idiot. Once when I was little, Grandma dragged me to Matt's hangout. She was spitting fire that day and determined to make an ass out of Matt for neglecting me.

When Grandma opened the door and we walked in, everyone at the smoky bar turned to look. Most of them were men, but there were a few women in the crowd. Grandma took my little hand and we walked to the end of the bar where Matt sat.

"Matt," Grandma said. "Don't you think you'd better come home? Your daughter needs you."

A woman sitting a few stools down from Matt looked at me. "I didn't know you had a kid, Matt. She's cute. Good thing she doesn't look a damn bit like you."

Everyone laughed.

"She's not mine," Matt said.

"Quit talkin' nonsense, Matt. She's as much you as you are me. Now get off your drunken ass, clean yourself up and come home."

Matt stood. "I told you once, Mom. I'm not going to tell you again. I don't want her. Take her. Do what you want with her. But never come in this bar again looking for me, telling me I need to be some kind of father. I'm not that man."

I ran up to Matt and kicked him as hard as I could in the shin. "I don't want you for a daddy."

"Son of a bitch, that hurt," Matt said. "You little…"

Grandma grabbed my hand and we practically ran out of the bar and we never went back – ever.

CHAPTER 27

"Now, Dad, when Cole gets here, don't ask him a million questions."

Tom looks up from his book. "Why are you telling me this and not your mom?"

"Because I know how you are."

Tom runs his fingers through his salt and pepper hair. "I just can't believe my little girl is going on a date."

"In case you haven't noticed, Dad, I'm not two anymore."

"But it's your first date, sweetie," says Elizabeth, tossing her *House Wonderful* magazine on the couch. "We just want to make sure that Cole's a nice boy."

"And responsible," Tom says. "Don't forget that. Not sure I should have given in and let you date him since he's a year older."

"Look, guys. I wouldn't be going out with Cole if he wasn't nice. And I think he's pretty responsible. At least he seems to be. He works hard in school and plays baseball. He's had to watch his little sister a lot over the years because of his parents' business."

"They run a bar, right?" Tom asks.

"Yes, Dad, a bar. They aren't professionals like you and Mom but that doesn't mean they're bad people."

"I don't think your father was saying they're bad people for running a bar."

"I know what he was thinking," Olivia says. "I could tell by the tone of his voice."

"Look, Lib," Tom says. "I'm sorry. I'm not a snob. You know that. It's just that I want the best for my little girl. That's all."

"Dad, this is our first date. It's not like we're getting married. Who knows? It could be our one and only date."

"OK. OK. I'll try not to ask too many questions."

"You know, Dad," Olivia says, "he'd like to be a doctor like you. You could talk to him about that. He's going to be the first one in his entire family to go to college. He has goals and plans and he's a hard worker and I know how much you value hard work."

Tom smiles and the doorbell rings.

"OK. That's him," Olivia says. "Remember, not too many questions."

Olivia picks up Daisy, who's at the door barking. She answers the door and, after introducing Cole to Daisy, leads him into the living room to meet her parents. Tom and Elizabeth stand.

"Mom. Dad. This is Cole. Cole, my mom and dad."

Cole extends his hand to shake their hands.

"So, Cole. Libby tells me you want to be a doctor."

"Yes, sir. I do."

"Good. Good. Get good grades, then?"

"I do all right."

"Gotta do better than all right to get into med school."

"Dad," says Olivia, with a clenched jaw.

"I just meant that med school is tough. Gotta work hard to make it through."

"I agree, sir," Cole says. "And I plan to."

"To what?"

"Work hard. Like you said."

"Libby tells us your parents own a bar," Elizabeth says.

"Yeah. It was my grandfather's."

"Where's it located?"

"Near the hospital, actually. On Broadway and Philadelphia."

"Are you Sam's son?"

"Yes, sir," Cole says. "You know my dad?"

"Had a drink or two in that bar in my younger days. We used to go there after work sometimes with the other residents. It was kind of our hangout. Remember that, Liz?"

Elizabeth nods. "Yeah, it's where we met. How could I forget Sam's Place? Do people still write on dollar bills and pin them on the walls and ceiling?"

Cole nods.

"The day we got engaged, we went to Sam's to celebrate with our friends. I wrote our names and the date with a black marker on a dollar bill and pinned it somewhere above the bar. Always wondered if that bill was still there. Haven't been there in years. Probably not since Olivia was born."

"Hate to cut short the reminiscing," Olivia says, "but we better leave if we're going to catch the seven-twenty show."

Tom, Elizabeth and Daisy watch as Cole opens the door for Olivia and she slips inside his Honda Civic and they drive away.

* * *

The first time Grandma met Bryan, she fired questions at him faster than popcorn popping. I thought for sure he would turn around and walk out. Talk about intense.

How old was he? Where did he live? What did he do? Did he go to church? Was he baptized? Why didn't he go to college? Did he ever get anything more than a speeding ticket? Who were his parents? Even I was stunned by some of her questions. Like if he was baptized. That's not something you ask a person the first time you meet. And, to be honest, I'm not sure it's a question I'd ever ask. I mean, who really cares? Well, Gram did. Big time.

I met Bryan at the grocery store where I worked. He always got in my checkout line, even though he could have used the express line because he only ever bought ice tea and thin pretzels. But he waited in my line no matter how long it was.

"So. How about going out sometime?" he asked one day. He shifted his weight from one foot to the other.

I could feel my face heating up. I was sure it was as red as the lady's lipstick behind him. I tried to speak but the words wouldn't come out. I felt as if I were trying to swallow a tennis ball and it got stuck in my throat.

He rubbed his neck. "Course, you probably have a boyfriend."

"Uh, no. It's not that. You just surprised me."

"Is that a yes?"

The woman with the red lipstick sighed. "Can you just give him your number, honey? I'm in a hurry. Gotta pick up my kid."

I wrote my number on the back of Bryan's receipt and handed it to him. He called the next day.

* * *

Traffic is heavy and Cole and Olivia arrive at the movie theater minutes before the show starts. They slip into the dark, crowded theater and find two seats in the back row next to a couple with tubs of popcorn and super-sized sodas.

Cole slips his arm around Olivia and she inches toward him. Olivia likes comedies and romances but Cole picked a thriller for their first date. When a scene is particularly bloody or violent, Olivia turns her face and buries it in Cole's chest. She's so close to his heart that she hears it beating. It reminds her of Lexie's party, when she laid her head on his chest for the first time and heard his beating heart.

She smiles, thinking about that night. How Lexie and Tallen went to Lexie's bedroom. How Tallen's other friends never showed up and Delaney, Molly and Jackie eventually left. And how she and Cole talked until three a.m., until she couldn't keep her eyes open any longer.

It was so easy to talk to Cole. So easy to open up to him and share her dreams and plans. He was different. He didn't try to make out. He hadn't even tried to kiss her, even though Olivia wanted him to. And when he asked for her number before he left, she couldn't write it down fast enough. Actually, she couldn't find a piece of paper so she wrote it on his wrist in blue pen. She noticed when he picked her up that the ink was faded but still there. And she wondered how long it would last before it was completely gone.

* * *

Bryan and I went to the movies on our first date, too. I don't remember much about the movie other than there was a lot of shooting and car chases. What I'll never forget is how I felt sitting next to him. I felt a strange tingling inside. It wasn't a bad thing, but it was scary because I had never experienced anything like it before. My body quivered when he reached for my hand and our fingers interlocked. This was the first time I had been this close to a boy and I wanted the sensation to last forever.

We stayed until the last credit rolled because Bryan wanted to see the extra scene they included at the end. As we left the theater he spotted a dime tails up in the parking lot. He reached down and turned it over.

"Aren't you going to pick it up?" I asked.

He smiled. "No, I turned it over to heads for someone else to find. Heads always brings good luck."

After the movie, we went for ice cream and sat in his Jeep and talked for hours. I was surprised at how normal and natural it felt to be with him. It reminded me of the box of gloves Gram brought home one fall day. Someone was cleaning out their closets and thought we could use them. I tried on one after another and finally found a pair. They weren't the newest pair or the best pair, but they fit perfectly.

I learned that Bryan lived alone, had no parents — he had avoided answering this question when Gram asked it and didn't want to go into details now — dropped out of high school but got his GED, worked at some warehouse on the loading dock and ran at least five miles every day.

"And, don't tell your grandma, but I don't think I've ever been baptized."

CHAPTER 28

"What am I supposed to do, Lib?" Cole asks. "I agreed to go to the prom with her before I met you."

Olivia and Cole have been dating for weeks and Olivia's upset because Cole is taking another girl to the prom.

"Does she know you have a girlfriend?"

"Yeah, I told her."

"And she still wants to go with you?"

"She's pissed, but she bought her dress and everything. It's not like we were a couple like you and me. It wasn't like that," Cole says. "She needed a date, I needed a date, and we were friends. Well, maybe she wanted to be more."

"Can't you get someone else to take her?" Olivia asks.

"All of my friends have dates. Look, we're just going to the prom. We'll eat, dance a little and leave."

"No slow dancing, right?"

"Right."

Olivia squirms closer to Cole. They are at her house watching a movie in the media room on the lower level.

"God, you're so beautiful," Cole says, brushing the curls off her face. He puts his hands on either side of her head and caresses her earlobes with his thumbs. Olivia closes her eyes and lifts her chin. He bends down to find her lips and their tongues tangle. "I love the way you kiss," he whispers.

"Then don't stop," Olivia says.

Olivia smells his woodsy cologne with a hint of musk and smiles. She bought it for him the other day while shopping with Lexie at the mall. The kiss deepens and she tastes the chocolate candy bar he ate moments before. The lights flicker and they stop and sit up. Olivia brushes her hair back with her hands.

"Everything all right down there?" asks Elizabeth from the top of the steps.

"Yes, Mom. We're just watching a movie."

The kids hear the door close and Cole finds Olivia's lips once again. She falls back on the sofa and pulls him on top of her and softly moans.

"God, Lib, we gotta stop." Cole sits up. "You're on fire tonight and I don't want to hurt you."

"But I like kissing you," she says.

"Well, I love kissing you. That's the problem. Stopping at kissing. You drive me insane inside. Christ, I've never been with a girl that makes me feel the way you do."

* * *

Watching Olivia and Cole make out is beautiful and frightening. I know they are falling in love. Since the party, they spend as much time together as they can. Olivia has dance and Cole has baseball, but what free time they have they spend with one another.

The first time Bryan kissed me I thought I was going to die. My entire body quivered and I just wanted more. I wanted someone to care about me my entire life and I finally found that in Bryan – or so I thought.

He didn't kiss me until the second date and then it was as if neither of us could get enough of each other. The kissing led to other things fast, things I had no idea about but Bryan taught me. He never made me feel incompetent or naïve. He led and I followed, learning as I went.

Sometimes, we'd drive an hour to the beach and just sit, side by side, listening to the surf pound the beach and watching the flat horizon swallow the blazing sun.

There was this private beach fronted by luxurious homes and we'd pretend that we lived in one of the mansions. We'd imagine what it looked like inside and describe certain rooms to each other.

Bryan always described a game room equipped with every gaming system ever made, pinball machines, pool, air hockey and foosball tables, a flat screen and a poker table. I'd usually describe a master bedroom with a gas fireplace, spa area, walk-in closets with tons of drawers and hooks and baskets to store things and a comfy reading area equipped with a flat screen mounted on the wall in case I wanted to watch TV.

Bryan was so easy to talk to and yet I always felt like there was something he was hiding, something that he was ashamed of. He never talked much about his family and when I asked, he'd somehow manage to change the conversation. He was good at that.

It was as if he had two lives, the one with me and the one that involved his work and home and family. I had never been to his apartment and he never asked me to go there. It was as if he wanted to keep that half of his life separate. I thought it was strange and yet it added a certain mysteriousness that appealed to me.

I was happier and more confident and able to shrug off Tracey Carmichael's nasty comments and actions more easily.

* * *

"Did you mean that?" asks Olivia, sitting up and straightening her top.

"Which part?" Cole says.

"The part where I drive you insane."

Cole smiles and nods. "Yes, Lib. I meant it."

"That's a good thing, right?"

"It's a dangerous thing."

"I thought you were a daredevil?"

"But I'm not stupid. And I don't want to hurt you."

"What if it's what I want?"

"Look, Lib. I'm crazy about you. These last few weeks you've turned my world upside down. But I don't want to hurt you. I want to take it slow."

"How many girls have you been with anyway?"

"Not going there," Cole says. "But I've never been with anyone like you. I never felt about any girl the way I feel about you."

"And how do you feel?"

I sensed the words were hanging on his tongue, ready to drop, but he was holding back, not wanting to scare Olivia. So, he changed the subject. "Ready to meet Lexie and Tallen for miniature golf?"

"We could cancel."

"Are you kidding me? And miss beating the two of them in one of the hottest matches of the year."

Olivia laughs. "OK. OK. You win."

* * *

Bryan and I played miniature golf once. We saw Tracey and Chase there. We were a couple of holes behind them. Chase waved but Tracey ignored us.

"Who's that?" Bryan asked.

"Tracey Carmichael and her boyfriend, Chase."

"That bitch from your school?"

"The one and only."

"Want me to whack my ball so it hits her?"

"Don't you dare. She's not worth wasting your time on."

"I wouldn't consider it a waste of time. I'd consider it a good use of my time."

"Bry, stop it."

"OK. OK. I won't do it."

Bryan kept his word but I noticed that he stared Tracey down every chance he got.

The next day in school, I overheard Tracey tell her minions in the locker room about seeing me and Bryan.

"She really has a boyfriend," Megan said.

"Yeah," Tracey said. "And he's hot. I can't imagine what he sees in the Goodwill..."

I came around the corner. "Girl. Actually, Tracey, he likes the hot, wild sex we have. He can't get enough of it."

That shut Tracey up. For the first time ever she had no comeback. Truth was, Bryan and I got to third base, but we always stopped before we went any further. Of course, Tracey didn't have to know that. Let her think I was the slut she always said I was. If I admitted it, maybe it would take the wind out of her sails.

* * *

Olivia and Cole get to the miniature golf course just as Tallen and Lexie pull in.

"So what's it tonight? Couples against couples or girls against guys?" Tallen asks.

"Let's do girls against guys," Lexie says. "OK with you, Lib?"

Olivia nods. They get their clubs and balls and head to the first hole. The course has a pirate's theme and includes a huge wooden ship that incorporates a couple of holes on its lower level and a couple on its top level.

As they play the course Lexie and Olivia discuss their plans to spend the night with their boyfriends. Lexie has told her parents that she's staying at Olivia's house and Olivia has told her parents that she's staying at Lexie's. In reality, they are spending the night at Tallen's house, whose parents are attending a corporate convention in Las Vegas.

"Everything set?" Lexie asks.

"I think so," Olivia says. "I don't think Mom and Dad suspect a thing."

"Look," Lexie says. "Don't do anything you don't want to do. Just because I'm sleeping with Tallen doesn't mean you have to sleep with Cole."

"I know that."

"Besides, I'm older."

Olivia laughs. "By one year. By the way, did you get them?"

"Yeah. Got the pills the other day. I went to the clinic downtown. No way was I going to my regular doctor. Definitely don't want my parents to know."

"What are you girls whispering about?" Cole asks.

Lexie snickers. "Wouldn't you like to know?"

"It's not nice to keep secrets," says Tallen, pulling Lexie toward him and kissing her.

"It's girl talk," Lexie says. "Stuff that you guys wouldn't be interested in."

"Wanna try us?" Tallen asks.

Lexie shakes her head. "Nah."

The guys win the game and they decide to pick up a pizza and take it to Tallen's house to eat.

"Anyone want a beer?" Tallen asks. Cole takes one but the girls stick with Diet Pepsi.

Tallen lives in a contemporary log home with a floor-to-ceiling fieldstone fireplace in the great room. It has six bathrooms and a theater, billiard room and custom bar on the lower level. A long lane lined with trees leads back to the home, which sits in the woods.

"Kind of dark back here," Olivia says.

"You get used to it," Tallen says. "We lived in a development like you and Lexie. Mom and Dad didn't like having neighbors so close. Out here, you can walk out in the backyard naked and no one will see you."

"Do you?" Lexie asks.

"What?"

"Walk out naked."

Tallen smiles. "No, but I have gone skinny dipping before."

"Hmm," Lexie says. "That might be fun."

"We'll be sure to try it when it's warmer," Tallen says.

* * *

I wondered what Tallen's parents did for a living. This place was amazing. I especially liked the log pergola in the back for outdoor entertaining.

I can't imagine what it would be like to live in Lexie's, Olivia's or Tallen's house. Each of them is beautiful yet different. They are the kind of houses Grandma and I used to look at in magazines while we were waiting in line at the grocery store. The kind Bryan and I would pretend we lived in at the beach.

Sometimes, when Grandma wasn't home and Bryan was over, I imagined what it would be like if we were married and it was our apartment. One time, Bryan and I were in my bedroom making out and Gram came home. He hid in my closet until she went to bed and then sneaked out.

* * *

Tallen and Lexie head for his bedroom, leaving Olivia and Cole alone.

"Do you ever think about it?" Olivia asks.

"Now what are you talking about?"

"Going all the way."

"Of course I think about it. Do you?" Cole asks.

Olivia nods.

Cole pulls her toward him. He kisses her top lip, then her bottom lip and her mouth opens and they fall into a deep kiss. The kind of kiss that is the beginning of so much more.

* * *

There are a lot of things I remember about Bryan. His strawberry-blond hair. The way his light brown eyes with gold specks danced. The way he made me feel as if I was the most important person in the whole world. He was the only guy in my entire life who loved me, who wanted me.

But the thing I remember most is the way he held me. I had never felt so safe in anyone else's arms. He was the shelter I had been searching for my entire life, the rock that I so desperately needed. I had never grown so close to anyone so quickly and I knew that it was more than just a crush. I felt with every part of my being that we were meant to be together, forever. That's why I gave myself to him. That's why when he left and Grandma died, I had no reason to live. That's what I thought, anyway. And then I realized too late that you can't let life take your life. You have to be strong.

CHAPTER 29

"I told you not to ride on his motorcycle," Tom yells at Olivia. "Now look at your leg."

Olivia burned her calf on the motorcycle exhaust pipe. The burn, about the size of a baseball, is painful and red and oozing.

"Sorry," Olivia says. "I should have listened."

Tom puts ointment on the burn and covers it with gauze. His voice is laced with anger and disappointment. "You know, Lib. Sometimes parents do know what they're talking about."

He points with his head to her neck. "When you get that?"

Olivia feels for Cole's class ring dangling on a silver chain around her neck. "Last night."

"How serious are you guys, anyway?" Tom asks.

Olivia's face turns red. "Dad."

"Don't Dad me. I was young once, too, you know. Look, Lib, you'll always be my little girl. Even when you're ninety. I want what's best for you. I like Cole. He has a good head on his shoulders. He's a hard worker. But he's heading into his senior year of high school and then has college. You still have a couple of years before college. Just don't get too serious too soon. You have your whole lives ahead of you."

He shakes his head and looks at Olivia's bandaged leg. "And damn it, no more motorcycle."

* * *

I remember Grandma having the same conversation with me about Bryan. Not the motorcycle part; the getting serious too soon part.

"You like that boy, don't you? A lot," Grandma said.

I nodded.

"Well, don't like him too much too soon. You have a couple of years of high school yet and I'm hoping you go to college."

"But, Gram," I said, "we can't afford college."

"I did some checking and you'll get a lot of financial aid because we don't have much money. For once, being poor counts for something. As long as you have the grades, you shouldn't have a problem. Course, you'll have to work part time during school, but the finance man at the college told me that there are jobs on campus. Like in the library or cafeteria."

"I can't believe you're already checking on college stuff."

"Never too early for that, Sarah. It'll be here before you know it. I want to make sure that you have the means to go if it's what you choose to do."

"What if I don't want to go to college?"

"You've seen the kind of life we have, barely scraping by, living from paycheck to paycheck. I thought you wanted better than that."

"I do."

"Well, education is what will get you there. Sitting around wishing for it won't make it happen. Buying a lottery ticket and hoping to win won't make it happen.

Not that I haven't tried that. Hard work will make it happen, and I expect you to work hard. Don't let me down, Sarah. Don't let me down like your dad did."

"First, Matt wasn't my dad. He provided the sperm that made me. That's it. So don't ever compare me to him. And, Gram, you got to know that I would never let you down on purpose. I love you. You've been wonderful to me all of these years. If it weren't for you, I would have ended up being raised in a stranger's home. So I'll try. I'll really try to do the best I can do to make you proud of me."

"That's all I've ever asked for," Grandma said. "Your best."

* * *

"So was your dad pissed when he saw your leg?" Cole asks.

"Very."

"He probably hates me."

"It's not your fault. I'm the one who didn't listen. I'm the one who touched the stupid hot muffler with my stupid leg. It's not like you made me do it."

"True, but I coaxed you into going on the cycle ride, knowing that your parents told you my cycle was off limits. I should have at least insisted that you wear long pants."

Olivia changes the subject. "Coming to the picnic tomorrow?"

"Wouldn't miss it."

Olivia's parents are having their annual Labor Day shindig and invited Cole's family.

"I told you my parents can't come, right? They're going away for their twenty-fifth anniversary."

"How romantic."

"Yeah. Dad surprised Mom. She doesn't know where he's taking her."

"Do you?"

"No, he wouldn't even tell me. All I know is that plane tickets are involved."

"I'll miss seeing you tonight," Olivia says.

"I'll miss you more. Wish you were hanging out with me instead of Lexie."

"I wish your stupid ass friend Tallen hadn't broken up with her and made her so miserable. What gives anyhow?"

"He's stupid — what can I say? Lexie is drop-dead gorgeous and lots of fun. Just between you and me, I think he really likes her – too much. It scares him because he's never liked anyone as much as he likes Lexie."

"He has a great way of showing it."

"He can't handle it so he's running," Cole says. "That chick he works with who's always coming on to him just made it easier."

"He's an asshole," Olivia says. "Lexie even went on the pill for him. I don't blame her for giving up on guys."

"You'd never give up on me, would you?" Cole asks.

"You'd never drop me, would you?"

"Not in a million years. I'm crazy about you."

"Even though we've never done it like Lexie and Tallen?"

"Lib, why do you get hung up on that so much?"

"Because I know you've been with other girls."

"But never with anyone like you. It will happen when the time is right. No pressure. No, 'We gotta do it because everyone else is.' I want it to be perfect for you."

* * *

Few things in life are perfect. I thought that Bryan was.

Turned out he vanished one day and I never heard from him again. It was as if he were a figment of my imagination, as if he never really existed. And yet I know that he did. The baby growing inside of me was proof of that. I knew that the night things got out of hand too fast and the condom sat unopened on my nightstand something would happen.

Grandma kept asking me where Bryan was. Why wasn't he coming around anymore or calling. Finally, I told Grandma that I didn't know. For the first time in a long time, Grandma held me as I cried in her arms.

I realized how little I actually knew about Bryan, how secretive he was about the part of his life that didn't include me. I didn't know where he lived. I didn't know where he worked. I didn't know where his parents lived, or if they were even alive. Come to think of it, I'm not sure if Bryan grew up here or moved here. Every time I'd ask these kinds of things, he'd change the subject or grow quiet. So after a while, I just stopped. It was better that way. And what did it matter anyway? The only thing that mattered was the present and our future. Of course, that's when I thought we had a future. That was before he left without even saying goodbye.

* * *

"Libby," Elizabeth calls. "Lexie's here."

Lexie finds Olivia in her room. She's sitting on her bed reading the newest issue of *Teen Entertainment*. Daisy is curled up beside her.

"Any good gossip?" Lexie asks.

Olivia looks up from the magazine. "Just the usual. I'm more interested in talking about you. How are you?"

Lexie looks at the door. "Mind if I close it?"

"Oh, sure."

As soon as Lexie closes the door she bursts into tears. She plops on the bed beside Olivia. "I hate him. I so hate him." She picks up the round brown throw pillow and punches it. "Asshole. Asshole. Asshole."

Daisy's ears perk up and she leaps off the bed and jumps up on the nearby couch, stretching out and resting her furry face on her paws.

Olivia hugs Lexie.

"What did Cole say? Anything?"

"He thinks Tallen likes you a lot. Like too much. And he's scared."

"Scared? Of what? It's not like I'm a vampire or some kind of evil person."

"I guess scared of caring too much."

"Come on, Lib. Really? Really? He said that? Sounds ridiculous. If he cared too much he wouldn't have done what he did."

Olivia hands Lexie the box of tissues sitting on the nightstand by her bed. "I don't know. It could make sense. From what Cole's told me, Tallen's never had a serious girlfriend. Never wanted a serious girlfriend. Then he met you and everything changed."

"Well, it changed for me, too. Before I moved here, I had lots of boyfriends. But Tallen was different. I know he had to feel it, too. And yet he breaks up with me. Tells me he doesn't love me anymore. Wouldn't even look me in the face when he said it. And then, as soon as he can, he changes his status on Facebook. Like he couldn't do it fast enough."

"Well, at least he didn't break up with you via text message like Molly's boyfriend did. He was an even bigger jerk."

"True," Lexie says. "But all guys are jerks. Who needs them anyway? You have the last non-jerkish guy. All the others suck big time."

"You'll get over him," Olivia says. "Mom and Dad say things always happen for a reason."

"Please, Lib. Don't give me that for-a-reason crap right now. That's what my mom said. Blah. Blah. Blah. It's all blah."

"So what do you want to do? Movies? Go to the mall? Eat a gallon of ice cream?"

"I guess mall. Dad let me take the new Benz and gave me his credit card and told me to have some fun. So let's go shopping. It's nice enough to put the top down. Screw guys forever!"

"Except Cole," Olivia says.

Lexie looks at her. "Except Cole. But he's the only exception."

Lexie pulls into the mall parking lot and parks near the entrance to the food court. As they walk toward the doors Olivia spots Tallen's car. She's hoping Lexie doesn't see it so she tries to distract her by talking about her upcoming dance recital.

Lexie stops and points. "There's Tallen's car. That freakin' jerk's here."

"Wanna leave?"

"Are you kidding me? He's definitely not going to stop me from shopping. The mall is my territory, not his. His is the…the…the stupid basketball court."

Olivia laughs to herself. Amused by how Lexie divides up public property with Cole.

"And another thing, the movie theater is mine. He never wanted to go to the movies until I started bugging him to go. So he can stay away from that, too."

The girls walk into the mall and head for Lexie's favorite store to look at the new fall arrivals.

They get lost in a forest of racks, going from one to another scavenging for that special something. Lexie holds up a black miniskirt and leopard-print shirt. "What do you think?"

Olivia walks around the rack so she's on the same side as Lexie. "Like it."

"Think it's sexy?"

"Definitely. Probably won't be able to wear it to school. Mini's too short."

"Stupid school dress codes," Lexie says. "Did I tell you I got sent home once because I had holes in my jeans? The jeans came that way. They were made that way, but Mr. Jerk-ass Principal didn't care. 'Rules are rules. Next time buy jeans with no holes,' he said. The guy has no fashion sense! Ever see his ties? They look ancient. Like something my dad would have worn thirty years ago."

"I think I'm ready to try these on," Olivia says.

"I'll be right behind you."

Olivia goes to the dressing room and sees Tallen walking with a girl she's never seen before. She's pissed that Tallen's in this store. He knows it's Lexie's favorite. If Lexie sees him she's going to go berserk. After all, in the dividing up of public property, this is definitely Lexie's territory. She turns to go back to get Lexie but she's too late. Lexie sees Tallen and the girl. They're laughing and headed in Lexie's direction.

Lexie walks up to them and before Tallen and the girl can say anything Lexie punches Tallen in the face. "This is my store, creep. So leave."

Tallen rubs his Brillo stubble jaw and the girl's brown eyes bug out. "Is this your crazy ex?"

"Yeah," Tallen says.

"Oh, I'm crazy all right. Crazy for ever liking this creep. Enjoy the crumbs I've left behind. It's probably all you'll get."

Lexie makes a beeline for the dressing room and Olivia follows her. As soon as they get inside a dressing room, Lexie melts into a puddle of tears. "I hate him," she says.

* * *

Hate is a strong word. I know how Lexie feels. To love someone so much and have them do the unthinkable. For me, Bryan vanishing from my life was like that. It was worse than breaking up. At least if he had broken up with me, I'd maybe still see him at the grocery store. But he cut off all contact with me. Whenever I had to work, I would look for him. Thinking that he might just pop in some day, tell me he was sorry and what the hell he had been up to all this time. But that never happened. The worst part is the not knowing. The not knowing what happened to him. Where he went. Why he left. So many questions that will never be answered. Not now, anyway. I'm dead. No chance of seeing him now. No chance of him ever knowing that I was carrying his child, the result of that unopened condom.

CHAPTER 30

Elizabeth knocks on Olivia's bedroom door.

"Come in."

Olivia notices her mom's red, blotchy face. "What's wrong?"

"Oh, Lib. I got some bad news today." Elizabeth sits on the edge of Olivia's bed.

Olivia gets up from her desk chair and walks over to her mom. I can feel Olivia's heart racing. She's scared. She's never seen her mom like this.

"What is it?" she asks.

Elizabeth pats the bed beside her. "Sit down, sweetie."

Olivia sits down.

"I have breast cancer."

Tears well up in Olivia's eyes. "Just like Grandma?"

"Yeah," Elizabeth says. "But you see how great Grandma's been. It's been twenty years since she had her mastectomy."

"Is that what's going to happen?"

Elizabeth nods. "I have cancer in my right breast. The surgeon will remove the breast and then I'll have chemo, just like Grandma. And, like Grandma, I'll be fine. I'll be tired and need lots of rest but Dad will see that you get to your dance classes."

"Oh, Mom," Olivia says. "I'm not worried about my dance classes. I'm worried about you."

"I know that, sweetie. But I'll be fine. You can't stop living your life just because I'm going through a difficult time. Bad things happen all of the time. You need to deal with the bad thing as best you can and move on. There are no guarantees in life. We do the best that we can."

Olivia hugs her mother tighter than she's ever hugged her. "Will I get breast cancer?"

"I don't know. I hope not."

"But if you and Grandma got..." Olivia catches herself. "Sometimes I forget," she says.

"You might be adopted, sweetheart, but you are my daughter," Elizabeth says. "You always have been and you always will be. No matter what. Yes, I did not give birth to you. But having a baby doesn't make someone a mother. I wish I knew more about your biological mother. I wish I knew her health history, but I don't. It's true, breast cancer runs in my family but it might not run in your biological mother's family. And even if it did, that doesn't mean you'll get it."

"I wish you had had me."

Elizabeth lifts up Olivia's chin. "It wouldn't have made any difference. I wouldn't have loved you any more than I do now. And you know you mean everything to your father. So, we'll get through this as a family just like we've gotten through every other difficulty we've faced. OK?"

Olivia blows her nose. "OK. But promise me you'll let me help, do whatever I can around the house."

"I promise."

"Mom," Olivia says. "I never want to lose you."

"You won't," Elizabeth says. "I'll always be with you. Even when I'm not physically here, I'll always be here." And she points to Olivia's heart.

Olivia covers her heart with both of her hands. "Forever and ever, Mom. Forever and ever."

* * *

If I were alive, I'd be melting in tears. Listening to Elizabeth talk to Olivia about her love for her fills me with incredible joy. My spiritual body tingles all over. It's a tingling brought about by a love so deep that even though I try to understand it, I'm not sure I do. I loved Grandma. I loved Bryan. But the love Elizabeth feels for Olivia, her adoptive child, is something so deep, so incredible that I can't relate to it. I can't help but wonder if I would have felt that way about the child I was carrying. And then I hate myself all over again. Hate myself for the choices I made, the things that I did. Hate myself for not being strong enough, for being so short-sighted that I couldn't see past tomorrow. When Bryan vanished and Grandma got sick, that was the beginning of the end.

I learned that Grandma was sick about a month after Bryan took off. By that time, I knew I was pregnant but there was no way I was going to tell Grandma and disappoint her. So I did what I always did. Hid it. It was easy to do. Just wore big shirts. I kept thinking that Bryan would come back and whisk me away and we'd be a family, but that didn't happen. Grandma just got sicker and sicker. And the baby inside of me grew bigger and bigger. I went to the clinic downtown for regular checkups. I wasn't sure what I was going to do so I didn't do anything. It was easier that way.

"Sarah," Grandma moaned from the recliner. "Can you bring me my pain pills?"

I set up the black TV tray with tole-painted roses beside her recliner. I put the remote on the tray along with a box of tissues and a water bottle filled with ice water.

"Here, Gram." I put the pain pills in her open hand. They looked so big I hoped they wouldn't get stuck in her throat. She had trouble swallowing big pills. Always did, but now it was even more difficult.

"Can you sit with me awhile?" Grandma asked.

"Sure, Gram." I sat on the floor next to her chair and laid my head on her thin legs, covered with my old pink and purple comforter that was threadbare in spots.

She brushed my hair with her boney, feeble hands. "I'm sorry, Sarah."

I looked up at her, taking in her sagging cheeks splattered with age spots and her thin, cracked lips that seemed to be vanishing. She had aged so much in three short months.

"Don't be sorry, Gram. You can't help you got sick."

"I don't want to leave you. I know where I'm going. I don't fear dying. But I don't want to leave you just yet."

"Oh, Gram," I said. "You'll be around another fifty years, and you'll be just as feisty as ever."

Her lips quivered and she managed a slight smile. "I don't have much, but what I have is yours."

"I'm not going to sit here, Gram, if you're going to talk dumb like this. You have pancreatic cancer. It's not the end of the world. You'll beat this just like you've beat everything else in your life. Aren't you always telling me to never give up, to keep on going even when things get tough? Isn't that what you've taught me? To fight until there's no more fight in you."

As soon as I said it I wished I could take it back, but it was too late. I knew what she was going to say and I didn't want to hear it.

"That's just it, Sarah. Your old grandma has no more fight left in her. Been fighting my entire life, and I'm just too damn tired."

"Sleep, Gram. I'll be back a little later to check on you."

* * *

Later that night, after her mother has gone to bed, Olivia finds her dad alone in the study. She hears his sobs. He doesn't realize he has company.

"Dad," Olivia says. "Are you OK?"

Tom turns around and wipes his eyes with the back of his hand. He sniffs. "I'll be OK, Libby Love. Just worried about your mom."

Olivia walks over to him and they hug. She notices an open bottle of Scotch on the desk and an empty glass next to it.

"Is Mom going to be all right?" Olivia asks.

Tom kisses the top of her head. "I hope, Lib. I really hope. But we have to be strong for her. Can't let her know how worried we are. I don't want her worrying about us when she needs to be taking care of herself."

* * *

"How's your mom?" Cole asks Olivia when she answers the door the next day.

"Sleeping now. She's tired a lot."

"Are you sure you can go out?"

"Yeah. Grandma's here and Dad will be home soon."

"Good cause we gotta celebrate."

Cole flashes his blinding white smile.

Olivia jumps up and down. "You got in."

"Yep."

She stands on tiptoe and hugs Cole. "That's awesome. I hope I get my first choice when it's time for me to apply to colleges."

"Any chance you'll apply to my school?"

Olivia shakes her head. "Need a school with a strong dance program."

Cole's shoulders sink. "But I can visit, right?"

Olivia smiles. "Of course."

She's happy when Cole talks about the future and refers to both of them. It makes her feel as if he thinks they're forever like she does.

"Where do you want to go to celebrate?" Cole asks.

"Pizza Palace," Olivia says.

"Could do Chinese?"

"Nah. Pizza. And then Tropical Treat for an ice-cream cone."

"You must be hungry," Cole says.

"You try dancing for six hours and see how tired and hungry you get."

"You don't get any breaks?"

"We get breaks, but not long ones and I eat very light because I don't feel well dancing on a full stomach."

Olivia leaves to tell her grandma that she and Cole are going.

"Almost forgot," Olivia says when she returns. "My parents are having my sweet sixteen birthday party at the club. They've booked the ballroom and hired a DJ. I need to decide the menu and who to invite. Wanna help?"

"Sure," Cole says. "How many people are you inviting?"

"Not sure. Dad said to invite whoever I want. So, I'll be inviting my dance friends and my school friends. And, of course, family."

"Sounds like it'll be fun."

"It's going to be amazing," Olivia says.

"What about your mom?"

"Mom insists. I told her we could wait to celebrate until after she's through with her chemo, but she said to go ahead, that with the party planner they hired she won't have anything to worry about. The only thing she asked was that we have it on the weekend right before she starts another round of chemo because that's when she always feels best."

* * *

When I turned sixteen, Grandma took me to this fancy restaurant in the swankiest hotel downtown. It was in the historic district, built in 1925. I remember looking at the menu and having no idea what most of the dishes were. Names like Assiette d'Agneau, Canard Rôti and Bifteck Diane stared back at me.

"There's no prices on my menu," I told Gram.

"Shh," she said. "Don't worry about the price. This is an extra special day. I've been saving a dollar a week for three years so that we could do this. Get what you want. You're sixteen."

"But I don't know what I want because I have no idea what any of these dishes are," I whispered.

When the waitress came, I asked her to explain the entrees. One was a lamb dish and the other duck. When she said "beef tenderloin" that at least sounded familiar. "I'll take that," I said.

I felt like royalty sitting in this dining room with its twenty-foot-high ceilings, ornate brass and crystal chandeliers and wood-paneled walls. A teen about my age walked around with a cold pitcher of water and it seemed like as soon as I took a few sips out of my glass he was beside me filling it up.

"Do you think we're dressed good enough?" I whispered.

We had worn our best clothes – I had on a blue silk dress that Gram had made me and she wore a floral dress that she only wore for very special occasions – but, compared to everyone else, we looked underdressed. I think the hired help looked better dressed than me and Gram.

"You're beautiful," Grandma said. "Only you can make yourself feel inferior. Don't. Our money is as good as theirs. And, gosh darn it, I've saved for three years to eat in this hotel and I'm gonna enjoy it."

Grandma told me on the taxi ride over — she said she couldn't afford a limo but a taxi would make us feel just as special — that she had always wanted to eat in this hotel.

"Ever since I was wee little," Grandma said. "We'd drive by it on our way to market and I'd see all these folks going in there all dressed up in suits and evening gowns. I used to pretend with my friend June that we were attending a ball there. Sort of like Cinderella."

I smiled. Gram always had a way of making something extra special. And I will never forget that night. We even had dessert.

Grandma got the Panko Crusted Chocolate Cheesecake, which was served warm with balsamic strawberry compote, and I got the Blueberry Upside Down Cake with house-made blueberry vanilla bean ice cream. Gram ordered the Thai Coconut tapioca with spiced mango salsa to go.

She winked. "We'll enjoy that tomorrow."

Neither of us said too much on the taxi ride home. We were too stuffed.

"Thanks, Gram," I said. "That was the best birthday ever."

Grandma smiled and wrapped her arm around me. "The best birthday for my best girl."

CHAPTER 31

"This is amazing," Delaney said. "The food, decorations, music. It must have cost a mint. And your dress. It's incredible."

"Think so?" Olivia twirls around in her black sequin strapless dress.

"Know so."

"Well, glad you're having a good time."

Delaney's eyes sweep the ballroom decorated in pink and black. Everything is perfectly coordinated, from the white tablecloths accented with fuchsia napkins to the white chair covers with fuchsia sashes to the black glass vases with fuchsia roses on each table. "Good time? How about the most awesome time ever?" Delaney says.

Olivia watches as Jackie pulls Delaney back onto the Italian marble dance floor.

Cole, also dressed in black, bends over to kiss Olivia. "She's right. This is one hell of a party your parents gave you."

"I know. Kind of feel bad about it. But it's what they wanted to do."

"Well, if they've done all this for your sixteenth birthday, I can only imagine what your wedding will be like."

Olivia bites her lower lip. "I was sort of hoping you'd be there for that."

Cole smiles and kisses her again.

"There you two are," Olivia's mom says. "Dad and I are heading home but you stay and enjoy yourselves. The party planner will oversee everything and make sure all of your gifts are taken back to the house."

"Are you OK, Mom?"

"Yes, sweetie. Just a little tired. There's just kids here now and Dad and I figured we'd let you and your friends party without us hanging around."

Olivia kisses her mom, who's wearing a silk black dress with a fuchsia headwrap. "Thanks, Mom. It was an incredible party. I will never forget it as long as I live."

"It did turn out rather well," Elizabeth says. "I especially liked the candy buffet."

The party planner had arranged a candy buffet that was filled with every kind of sweet imaginable – from homemade chocolates to hand-dipped cake pops. Each guest was given a tin – custom ordered with Olivia's picture on it – to take to the candy buffet and fill. It was Olivia's gift to them.

Olivia's dad, dressed in a black suit and fuchsia tie, walks up. "I see you found our birthday girl."

"I was just telling her that we're going to head home and that she and her friends can stay another hour," Elizabeth says.

"That OK with you, Lib?" Tom asks.

"Of course, Dad. And thank you for the wonderful party. You're the absolute best."

"Nothing's too good for my little girl," says Tom, kissing Olivia on the forehead.

"Will you dance with me before you go?" Olivia asks.

"You bet," Tom says. "What should I tell the DJ to play?"

"Surprise me."

Tom talks to the DJ and whisks Olivia out onto the floor. The DJ announces that Olivia and her father will dance and the guests clear the area.

Cole sits with Elizabeth and watches. "Daddy's Little Girl" blares from the speakers and Olivia and her dad float across the floor, from one side to the other and from end to end.

"I would never be able to dance like that," Cole whispers to Elizabeth.

"Sure you could. It just takes practice. I'm sure Libby would teach you."

Elizabeth opens her purse and takes out a tissue and dabs her eyes.

"You OK, Mrs. K?"

Elizabeth smiles. "Yes. Happy, that's all."

* * *

I can't describe how it felt to watch Tom dance with Olivia. Moments of the two of them over the years flashed before me. Tom holding her for the first time. Tom singing to her. Rocking her. Feeding her. Crawling around on all fours with Olivia on his back. Bringing home yet another stuffed animal. Picking her up and twirling her around as she giggles. Tucking her in bed at night.

Olivia was so lucky to have Tom as a father. If Matt ever held me, I was too young to remember. He never sang to me or rocked me or fed me. Or tucked me in at night. It was Gram who did all that. Gram who was my mother and my father, who even as she lay dying was more concerned about me than about herself.

I realized that that's the kind of love that can't be bought or sold. You can't barter for it or bid on it. It just is. And those who realize the power of love realize that with it, anything's possible.

"Sarah," Grandma said one day. "When I'm gone..."

"Don't talk like that, Gram."

She looked at me with tired eyes. They seemed to be closed more often than they were open these days. The extra skin on her eyelids sagged more than usual and it seemed as if the wrinkles that creased her face had deepened and multiplied overnight.

"When I'm gone..." she licked her dry, caked lips "...don't spend a lot of money on a gravestone. I don't need one. That marker the funeral home puts in the ground will be just fine."

"Gram, seriously. Stop it."

"And bury me in that floral dress I only wear for really special occasions. You know the one. I wore it when we went to that fancy restaurant to celebrate your sixteenth birthday."

"Gram."

She looked at me and narrowed her eyes. "You take whatever money we have and you go to college. OK?"

"I'll think about it."

"Sarah, I mean it. I talked to Mr. Little. He'll take care of this old body when I'm done with it. Just call him. He knows what to do."

I stopped listening to Gram. I felt the life inside of me kick and I just couldn't imagine having this child without Gram or Bryan. I didn't know if it was a boy or girl. All I knew was that I couldn't be its mother – alone. And if I couldn't be its mother, then what was I going to do?

There were times when I wanted to tell Gram everything. Times when I needed to tell her. Needed her advice or words of wisdom. But I didn't say anything. She was too sick and there was no way I was going to give her more troubles to think about.

Even at school I was more quiet than normal. I don't know if Tracey Carmichael was growing out of her meanness or if she just stopped caring about me, but even she wasn't hassling me as much.

* * *

Cole and Olivia say goodbye to the last guest and head to the car.

"Did you notice how much Lexie and Bryce danced?" Olivia says. "Seemed to be some fireworks there."

"Really? I hadn't noticed."

"How could you not notice? Every time there was a slow song, Bryce and Lexie danced. He didn't let anyone else get near her."

Cole opens the car door for Olivia. "Only girls notice that kind of stuff."

Olivia turns toward Cole. "Did you notice the dress Ann was wearing?"

"Yes. Now that I noticed."

Olivia hits him. "Figures! Now how could you notice that and not notice Lexie and Bryce dancing to every slow song?"

"Uh. I don't know."

"Could it be because there wasn't much to Ann's dress?"

"Uh. I hadn't noticed."

"Seriously, Cole. Fess up."

"Well, it was pretty revealing. I thought for a minute that she had one of those boob jobs."

"For the record, no boob job. I think she was wearing a push-up bra."

"A what?"

"Push-up bra. It's padded and makes your breasts look bigger. They make some that add two sizes."

Olivia climbs in the car and Cole walks around to the other side and gets in.

"You know, Lib, that was a great party. And you were the most beautiful girl in the whole place."

"Nice recover."

"No, seriously." He reaches and brushes the blonde curls off her face, dusted with sparkly glitter. "I love everything about you and I love that you love me."

Instinctively they lean toward one another and fall into a deep kiss.

I remember the first time Cole told Olivia that he loved her. They were sitting on swings in Olivia's backyard. Stars blanketed the sky and Olivia pointed out the Big Dipper. Cole explained that the Big Dipper is formed from the seven brightest stars in the constellation Ursa Major, or Great Bear. And that according to Greek mythology, Zeus' wife, jealous over his lust for a woman named Callisto, turned her into a bear. Callisto, while in bear form, encountered her son and just as he was about to kill her, not realizing it was his mother, Zeus hurls them both into the sky forming Ursa Major.

"How do you know such random stuff?" Olivia asked him.

They twisted their swings so they were facing each other.

"Here's something I know that's not random. Something I've wanted to tell you for a long time."

Olivia bit her lower lip and tilted her head so her long curls cascaded down her left shoulder. Cole took her hands in his.

"I love you, Lib."

And they kissed and got carried away and fell off the swings. Daisy, who had been chewing a bone nearby, started to bark at the commotion.

I will never forget that moment. It's one I'll show Olivia at the end.

* * *

"I better get you home," Cole says. "I promised your mom and dad we wouldn't be out late. But, I do want to give you my gift."

Cole hands Olivia a long rectangular box. She peels back the pink and silver swirly paper, folding it to save. She opens the box and her jaw drops.

"It's beautiful, Cole." She lifts the silver heart-shaped pendant encrusted with small diamonds out of the box.

"Are you sure you like it?"

"No." Olivia pauses. "I love it. Can you put it on?"

Olivia turns her back to Cole and he puts it around her creamy neck and fastens it. He kisses the nape of her neck. "God, you're beautiful."

She turns around to find his lips once more and eventually they head home.

* * *

Bryan gave me a heart pendant once. Of course, it was nothing like the one Cole gave Olivia. I'm pretty sure those were real diamonds. I saw the necklace Bryan bought me at a boutique in the mall. Still, I loved that necklace. It was the first and only time a guy ever gave me anything. It, too, was silver. No diamonds, though. Not even fake ones. But it was beautiful and I never took it off. Well, not until the end anyway.

Bryan was so excited the day he gave me the necklace. He picked me up after my shift at the grocery store. When I got in his car, I noticed his I-got-a-secret grin. It was the one where his closed mouth was higher on the left and pushed his cheek into his eye making his eye squint.

"Why are you grinning?" I asked. "You look like you're up to something."

"There's something for you inside the glove box."

I looked toward the box.

"Go ahead. Get it."

I opened the glove box and found a long, rectangular gift wrapped in newspaper. I took it out. "Want me to open it now?"

Bryan nodded. I could tell he was happy. His eyes danced in the moonlight that seeped through the car windows. He held his breath while I tore off the paper and lifted the lid.

"Bryan, it's beautiful," I said, taking the necklace out of the box.

"I just wanted you to know that you'll always have my heart, even when I'm not with you. This is a reminder."

Tears gathered in my eyes. It was such a lovely thing to say and I wondered if he had practiced it much or if it just came to him. Either way I felt loved and wanted, which was why it was so hard for me when Bryan ditched me. No phone call. No last-minute visit. Nothing. How can you love someone so much and then just leave? Maybe that's it. Maybe he didn't love me as much as he said he did. Or maybe I made more of it than what was there.

As cruel as Tracey Carmichael had been to me my entire life, what Bryan did hurt me so much more. And the life growing inside of me each day was a reminder of the love we had and the love that was gone, to where I had no idea. All I knew was that it wasn't with me.

I kept the necklace on, mostly out of hope that he would show up one day and tell me what a big jerk he had been. But he never showed up.

CHAPTER 32

Olivia jumps up and down in front of her mom, who is wearing a Bohemian floral head wrap instead of one of her custom-made wigs.

"So you really mean it, Mom? You're better?"

"That's what the doctor says. Everything is looking good."

"How should we celebrate?" says Olivia, hugging her mom.

"That's what I wanted to talk to you about."

"I'm all ears, Mom."

"Dad and I were thinking about going away for the weekend."

"Like where? And can Lexie come?"

Elizabeth bites her lip. "Dad and I were thinking that just we would go away."

"No problem. You're right. It should be a family thing. No Lexie."

"Look, Lib," Elizabeth says. "You know Dad and I love you. You're the most important person in the whole world to us. But, well, we were thinking that just maybe the two of us would go away. You know. Kind of like a couple."

Olivia hits her forehead with the palm of her hand. "Why didn't you say so? Of course. Not a problem. Yes. Just you and Dad. How romantic."

"I was hoping you'd say that. We haven't gone away for a weekend, just the two of us, since you came into our lives. And, well, with the cancer and all. Dad just thought that maybe it's about time we did. Plus you're older. Grandma said she would come over if you wanted her to."

"Mom. I'm sixteen. I think I can take care of myself for a few days. I think a romantic getaway is just what you and Dad need. It doesn't take a doctor to know that you both have been super stressed lately and need some time alone to reconnect and unwind. Besides, I'm sure Lexie will come over if I ask her."

I knew that Olivia had no plans to ask Lexie. As soon as she understood what her mom was trying to tell her and realized she would have the whole house to herself, something that had never happened, her mind shifted to Cole. How she could cook him a romantic dinner, hang out all night, watch their favorite movies and make out.

"So you're sure you're not mad?" Elizabeth asks.

Olivia is lost in her daydreams.

"Lib?"

"Oh, what? What?" Olivia says. "Did you say something?"

"I just want to make sure you're not mad."

"I'm not mad, Mom. I'm happy. Happy that you're better. Happy that you and Dad are going away for the weekend. Happy that you adopted me and raised me and love me with all your hearts. Happy that I have the two best parents in the whole world."

"You know, Lib, when we got you our lives changed forever. We had hoped for a child for so long. Dad wanted to name you Hope because you were everything we had hoped for. I had promised my grandmother that if I ever had a daughter I would name my daughter after her. So, you became Olivia Hope."

"How come you didn't tell me that before?" Olivia asks. "I mean, I knew I was named after your grandmother, but I didn't know the Hope part, that Dad picked that name and why."

"Well, now you know, sweetie. You're everything and much more than we had hoped for."

"Mom," Olivia says, "I love you so much." And she hugs her mother so tightly Elizabeth coughs.

* * *

If I had lived and had a daughter, I would have named her after Grandma, which means she would have been named Grace. And I would have given her my mom's first name as her middle name, so she would have been named Grace Sue. I love that it pays respect to the two most important women in my life – the woman who gave her life for mine and the woman who raised me.

It took Grandma dying to finally tell me about my mom and my birth. How my mom had a lump on her back. How by the time she went to the doctors to have it checked, she was pregnant with me. How it was melanoma, the deadliest type of skin cancer. How the doctors told her that they could try to save her but it meant she would have to abort me. How Matt pleaded with her to get rid of me. Told her that they could have other babies. That she had to have the chemo. But she refused.

And so, as I grew in her, she grew weaker and weaker. By the time my due date approached, Grandma said my mom was bedridden. Her days dwindling. The end came much more quickly than anyone had expected. Mom was whisked into a bay in the emergency room on a sunny summer morning and delivered me via Caesarean and then died.

I asked Grandma if my mom saw me before she died. If she knew I had lived. Neither Gram nor Matt was allowed in the room while I was born. Everything was going wrong and the doctors didn't want them in the way, Grandma explained.

"But," Grandma said, "there was a nurse there and she came to visit a few weeks later. Said she'd been having trouble sleeping. Felt awful about your mom and you. Just had to see you. And she told me that she was right beside your mom when you were born and that the doctor laid you on your mom's chest and that your mom felt you against her skin and smiled and then died. Just like that. She was waitin' for you to be born. Making sure you were gonna be all right. And as soon as she knew, she stopped fighting to live and went to where she needed to go."

Now that I know about moment keepers, I wonder about my mom. Who she's keeping moments for. Or if she even has someone yet. Wendy told me that moment keepers don't always return right away like me. Some wait years. It all depends on the great matchmaker. He decides who is going to be a moment keeper for whom and it's not always who you think it might be or should be. Most times, Wendy said, there's no relationship to the person in real life. I didn't know Wendy. She wasn't a relative or a neighbor. I had never even seen her before. And yet she was chosen for me for some reason. A reason I'm sure became known to Wendy at some point, or maybe not until the end.

* * *

"Hey, guess what," Olivia tells Cole while she's supposed to be studying in her room. "Mom and Dad are going away for the weekend. The whole weekend."

"Does that mean what I think it means?"

"Yep. Whole house to myself. And did I say all weekend?"

Olivia draws out "all" for emphasis.

"So what do you have planned?" Cole asks.

"For starters, I'll make you dinner on Saturday. I make a pretty wicked cheese omelet."

"I like wicked. Then what?"

"Then we'll have dessert. What do you want?"

"For dessert?"

"Yeah."

"You."

Olivia giggles. "I think I can arrange that."

The teasing continues for a few minutes until Olivia hears a knock at her door and her mom's voice.

"Gotta go. Mom's coming."

Olivia tosses her cell phone aside and picks up her book. "Come in."

Elizabeth cracks the door and peeks in. "What's ya reading?"

Olivia shows her the cover.

"*The Catcher in the Rye.* Now that's a classic," Elizabeth says. She walks over and sits on Olivia's bed.

Olivia pinches the few remaining pages. "Almost done, see?"

"What do you think?" Elizabeth asks.

Olivia shrugs her shoulders. "OK, I guess. Hey, the part I just read reminded me of that carousel you and Dad used to take me to when I was little. It was at a park near Grandma's house."

"The one with the brass ring?" Elizabeth asks.

"Yeah, that one. I used to love that carousel. Remember how I always wanted an outside horse so I could reach for the brass ring when the bell rang and that metal arm came out?"

"I remember. There were many times I thought you'd fall off that horse you were leaning so far off of it, holding on with one hand and one foot in the stirrup."

Olivia smiles. "But I got the brass ring. Once."

"Yes, you did."

"What ever happened to that old carousel anyway?" Olivia asks.

"When the park closed, the carousel was disassembled and sold to another park. There aren't too many golden carousels around anymore."

"I'd like to go on that carousel again sometime. Maybe get the brass ring."

* * *

I know exactly the grand carousel Olivia is talking about. I can hear its bellowing band organ and see its beautiful antique, hard-carved horses going round and round. When I was little, Grandma took me to that same amusement park and I rode that same carousel. Gram told me it was built around 1913 and that she rode it when she was a kid. I remember getting seven steel rings once, reaching out and grabbing them with my right hand and ringing them around my left index finger. Never got the brass ring, though. Not once.

Funny the things you forget and then when you remember them they come back to you in full color. I can see myself on top of the prancing white horse with its gold, red, white and blue saddle and harness. I always sprinted to get this horse with its front two legs in the air and the back two on the ground. It was so much better than riding the tattered and chipped coin-operated one in front of the old grocery store in town. That one was tan with a brown saddle and all four of its legs were in the air so I felt like I was galloping. Still, it couldn't compete with the white horse and a chance to grab the brass ring.

CHAPTER 33

Olivia pulls into her driveway and puts the car in park.

"Are you sure you're going to be OK staying alone in the house?" Olivia's grandma asks.

"I won't be alone. Daisy'll be here."

"Well, if you change your mind and want me to come over, just call. I left tonight open just in case."

"Grandma," Olivia says. "I'll be fine. Don't worry. And thanks for letting me drive. I need all the practice I can get since Mom never takes me driving. Says it makes her too nervous."

"I thought she had hired a driving instructor?"

Olivia nods. "She did, but lessons haven't started yet. The only day I don't have dance is Sundays so that's when they'll have to be."

Olivia grabs her dance bag and gets out of the car. Her grandma walks around to get in the driver's side.

"Sure you don't want to come in?" Olivia asks.

"No. I promised Grandpa that I'd stop at the store on the way home and get him the spice he needs for the soup he's making."

Olivia kisses her grandma. "Thanks for taking me."

"Any time, sweetheart. And remember, call if you need me."

Olivia opens the back door to find Daisy waiting just inside. She reaches down to pet her. "OK, girl. I'm home. Let's go out and pee."

Olivia grabs Daisy's leash and takes her out. Daisy spots a rabbit in the yard and takes off after it, pulling Olivia behind. Olivia slips on the grass and falls on her butt just as Cole comes around the corner.

"Daisy!" Olivia yells. "Bad."

Cole runs to help her up. "You OK?" He takes the leash with one hand and helps Olivia up with the other.

"Dang Daisy," Olivia says. "I could have twisted my ankle or worse. Then I really would have been screwed."

"That's right. You have that big dance thing next week," Cole says.

"It's called a recital," Olivia says. "And remember you said you'd come."

"I promise I'll be there," says Cole, following Olivia into the house and removing Daisy's leash. "So how was dance anyway?"

"Great. We focused on lyrical dance and my teacher commented on my leaps. Said they were 'exceptionally high' and that she was pleased."

Cole follows Olivia to the couch. She sits down and pulls him next to her. He brushes her soft curls off her face. "You really love dance, don't you?"

"More than anything," Olivia says. "It's all I've ever wanted to do. When I was little, I used to dream of performing Swan Lake with the New York City Ballet at the Lincoln Center. I used to beg my parents to move to New York just to be near the theater so I could go all the time."

"Your face lights up when you talk about it. Like you would never be happy unless dance was a part of your life."

"I wouldn't. Which is why I'm studying and practicing so hard. Next year at this time, I'll be auditioning for Juilliard. They have a great dance program that incorporates classical ballet and modern dance."

"Well, Lib," Cole says. "From what I've seen, I'm sure you'll make it. Someday, I'll see your name up in lights in New York City's theater district."

Olivia smiles and lays her head on his chest and he slips his arm around her and pulls her in. "What about you? What's your dream?"

"You know I've always been interested in medicine. Been thinking lately that it would be kind of nice helping kids, so maybe be a pediatrician."

"I could totally see you doing that," Olivia says. "I've seen you around your little cousins and you're amazing with them. If you end up at NYU, I could visit you and we could go to the theater together. Wouldn't that be nice?"

"Which part?"

Olivia hits him with her elbow. "Both parts."

"You visiting me, definitely. Going to the ballet, well, let's just say I'd choose something else to do."

"Like what?"

"Like this."

Cole finds Olivia's lips and they kiss deeply. She falls back on the couch and he eases on top of her. She wraps her arms around his back, running her fingers through his thick, dark hair. He kisses the corner of her mouth, making his way along her jaw line to her ear. He nibbles on her earlobe and she lets out a soft moan.

He tucks a strand of hair behind her ear. "Did I tell you I love you lately?"

Olivia smiles. "Not today."

"God, Lib. I love you." He kisses her temple and forehead and finds her lips again. "We'd better stop. You're making me crazy."

Olivia smiles. She unbuttons his jeans. .

"Lib, I mean it. Don't tease me like this."

"Who said I'm teasing?"

"But we talked about this. We decided to wait and I didn't bring anything with me."

"One time won't hurt," Olivia says. "Besides, who knows when we'll get a chance like this again?"

She puts her hands on his face and pulls it toward her. She kisses his upper lip, then his lower lip before their tongues find one another again.

"OK," Cole says. "But not here. Not on the couch. I want your first time to be comfortable."

"Then let's go to my bedroom," Olivia says.

Cole gets off Olivia and she takes his hand and leads him upstairs. Daisy, curled up on the chair opposite the sofa, has been watching. She lifts her head and jumps off the chair and follows them upstairs, only to be shut out of the room when Olivia closes the door.

Olivia whips back the soft comforter and turns to face Cole. She stands on her tiptoes to kiss him before unbuttoning his shirt and slipping it off his arms. She kisses his chest and works her way down to his belly button. She finds his zipper and just as she works it down the phone next to her rings. It's the landline that has been in her bedroom forever. Olivia glances at the number and sees it's her parents.

"Shit, I gotta get this. It's Mom and Dad."

Cole pulls up his zipper and sits on Olivia's bed.

"Hi, Mom. Dance was great. No, Grandma didn't stay. I'm fine. Daisy's here with me. How about you? Having fun?"

By the time Olivia gets off the phone with her parents the romantic moment has evaporated.

"Sorry about that," Olivia says.

"Probably for the best anyhow," Cole says.

"Want to pick up where we left off?" Olivia asks.

"Actually, Lib, I'm hungry. How about that wicked cheese omelet you promised me?"

* * *

I have to admit, I was relieved when Olivia's phone rang. While I had watched them make out many times, there was something about this time that scared me. For the first time, I felt as if Olivia would give herself to Cole completely. I knew the first time I saw her with him that it was only a matter of time, and I thought that time had come. Thanks to the phone call, it was put off a bit longer. But how long, I wasn't sure.

The first time Bryan and I made love, we were in the middle of an orchard between two rows of peach trees. It was a hot, muggy August night and we spread the old tattered blanket he kept in the trunk of his car on the ground. Bryan had picked fruit at this orchard growing up and knew how to get to this spot without being seen.

A crescent moon hung in the night sky, dotted with stars, some brighter than others. Bryan put punk sticks in the ground around the blanket. When he lit them, the smoke kept the bugs away. I hated bug bites more than anything.

We didn't plan on going the whole way. We just planned to make out, maybe go to third base. But then one thing led to another and the next thing I knew we were tangled together completely. Inseparable and it felt completely right. But, like Olivia, I wasn't ready. Bryan wasn't ready either. And, well, let's just say that things can happen when you're not ready.

* * *

Olivia flips the omelet in the cast-iron frying pan. "What kind of cheese do you want? American or Swiss or Muenster?"

"Swiss. Are you sure you don't want me to help?"

Cole sits at the table checking sports scores on his cell phone.

"No. It's almost done. Wheat or white toast?"

"Wheat. With some mustard."

Olivia divides the omelet and slides half onto wheat toast for Cole and half onto white toast for her and carries it over to the table along with the mustard.

"That looks amazing," Cole says.

Olivia sits down across from him. "Told you I could make a wicked omelet. The trick is to add a little milk, just enough to make the omelet light and fluffy. And to use a whisk to mix it. Not a fork."

"I didn't know you were so domestic," Cole says.

"There's probably some other things you don't know about me."

"Like what?"

"Like my favorite color is pink."

"I knew that. Even if you hadn't told me I'd know because you wear so much of it."

"True," Olivia says. "OK. Here's something you didn't know about me. I was adopted."

Cole's eyebrows arch. "I had no idea. How come you never told me that before?"

Olivia shrugs. "I don't know. I don't talk about it much. It's not that I'm ashamed of it, but it's just that when I think about it, it hurts a little. To think that my birth mom didn't want me. Luckily for me I ended up with the best parents in the entire universe."

"Ever wonder about your birth mom? Enough to find out more, I mean?" Cole asks.

"I thought about it, but only briefly. I wouldn't want to do that to my mom and dad. I wouldn't want them to think that I don't love them. I know that they wanted a baby for a long time before I came into their lives and when they finally got me, it was a dream come true. At least that's what they've always told me. Still, I do wonder what she was like. If I look like her. If she loved to dance as much as me. That sort of thing."

Cole sips his Coke and takes another bite. "Well, you ended up with a great family."

"True. Now your turn."

"For what?"

"Tell me something I don't know about you."

Cole scratches his head. "Not sure there's anything that would really surprise you."

"It doesn't have to surprise; it can be anything."

"OK. I got something. I had hernia surgery when I was in fourth grade."

"Ouch. Did it hurt?"

Cole shakes his head. "Not really."

"How did you find it?"

"Well, don't laugh. But my balls, er, scrotum, got big. I thought I was dying. I didn't want to show my mom so I showed my dad."

"It was that big?"

"Yeah. Bulging."

"Some girl in my dance class had a hernia once," Olivia says. "She showed me the bulge in her upper stomach. I think she strained herself lifting weights or something. Got anything else good?"

Olivia and Cole continue sharing. I learn that Cole was an altar boy, that his favorite book is *The Count of Monte Cristo* — despite its length — that he has a black belt in Tang Soo Do, that his favorite cereal is

Frosted Flakes and that if he could pick anywhere in the world to vacation it would be Rome, Italy — he loves studying the great Roman Empire and he could totally live on pasta and gelato.

* * *

Watching the two of them exchange likes — and dislikes — made me realize how very little I knew about Bryan.

I couldn't tell you what his favorite food was or his favorite vacation — if he even went on vacation — or his favorite TV show or movie. Odd that you can be so close to someone and not know basic stuff like their favorite TV show or food. Or where they live or work.

It's the reason why when I went looking for him I couldn't find him. I didn't know where to even begin to look. Guess he wanted it that way. Probably figured he was going to use me and then ditch me when he got bored. That's probably why he kept everything to himself. Why else would someone just stop calling, stop coming around, drop out of your life completely? It's the only thing that makes sense. There's no other explanation.

* * *

Cole helps Olivia put the dishes in the dishwasher. "Want to pick up where we left off upstairs?" he whispers into her ear.

Olivia puts her arms around Cole's neck and he bends down to kiss her. I feel the intense feelings Olivia has for Cole, that deep euphoric feeling of love that consumes her. I feel her heart flutter and the tingling feeling that pervades her tiny teenage body with a yearning so deep and a curiosity so raw it stuns me. And yet I fear for her, fear that she's not ready, not thinking as clearly as she should. But I can't stop her and Cole. All I can do is watch and record.

I'm embarrassed by being part of such a private moment. To watch them clumsily undress and make out and then, just when I think I should look away, it happens. I feel a stabbing pain and I gaze at Olivia's face, looking for a sign she's OK. And then I see it even before she does. The sheet is covered with blood.

CHAPTER 34

Lexie flops on her bed. "I can't believe summer is over. I'm so not ready to go back to school. Did I tell you Tallen called? He wants to get back together."

"What'd you tell him?" Olivia asks.

"Told him he's crazy and that I have a new boyfriend."

Olivia curls up on the lime-green papasan chair. "You didn't tell me about anyone new."

"That's because there's nothing to tell because there really isn't anyone new. I just made that up. Screw Tallen. I wouldn't go out with him if he were the last person alive on earth. He sucks at kissing and isn't smooth at all when it comes to the moves, know what I mean? Talking about making out, what's up with you and Cole? You've been acting weird ever since that weekend your parents went away."

I know that Olivia wants to talk to Lexie. She's been scared and Lexie's right, Olivia's been moody and distant. Even her parents have noticed it.

"Your mom and dad aren't home, right?" asks Olivia, her left eye and thumb twitching.

"Nope, it's just us. And when they do come home, we'll know because we'll hear the garage door go up. So go ahead, Lib. Tell me what's wrong."

Olivia bursts into tears. "Everything's wrong."

Lexie jumps up and grabs the box of tissues on her nightstand. "It can't be that bad, Lib."

"Trust me, it is."

In less than sixty seconds Lexie knows the entire story.

"And we were just making out, you know. Didn't plan on going the whole way. Well, maybe we thought about it but I don't think either of us really planned to go quite that far. And then we did. And it hurt and blood was everywhere. We took off the sheets and filled my bathtub with cold water and soaked the sheets in the cold water to get the blood out before washing them. And then we scrubbed the mattress with Comet that we found under the bathroom sink because the blood had seeped through the sheets and onto the mattress and there was a big white spot where we scrubbed so we turned the mattress over because Mom changes my sheets usually and I didn't want her to see the big, bleached spot. And it hurt and I cried and Cole was upset because I was crying and I haven't gotten my period yet and we only did it this one time but what if I'm pregnant?"

Lexie bit her lip-glossed lower lip. "Calm down. We'll figure this out. Let's just take one step at a time. One time I didn't get my period and it was just late. That's probably what it is. You're just late because you're worrying so much about getting it. We'll go to the drug store and buy a pregnancy test."

Olivia buries her head in her narrow hands. "There's no way I can walk into a store and buy one of those things."

"I'll buy it. You can even wait in the car if you want. I've bought one before — it's no big deal."

"But I thought you were on the pill?"

"I am, but one time..." Lexie pauses, as if she's contemplating whether she wants to tell Olivia her story. "Just believe me when I say I used one before."

Olivia looks at Lexie, curious to know when but respecting her friend's privacy enough not to ask.

"Look, Mom and Dad said they'd be late," Lexie says. "Something about a dinner party at one of Dad's clients, so I think we have all night. We'll go get the test and then come back here."

* * *

I remember the day I bought a home pregnancy test. My periods weren't real regular and I wasn't good about keeping track, but one day it occurred to me that I hadn't gotten my period for a while.

I was preparing a bath for Grandma and when I looked in the vanity below the sink in the bathroom to get some bubble bath, I noticed the box of tampons, which reminded me that I hadn't used any in a while.

And then I thought about how tired I had been and how queasy I felt, especially in the morning right after I woke up. I Googled pregnancy symptoms and saw that I had many of them, including tender breasts. That was when I went to a store on the other side of town so I wouldn't run into anyone I knew. I did it in the bathroom, and, when I saw the plus sign pop up almost instantly, I cursed Bryan, who by this time had stopped calling or coming by.

I couldn't tell Grandma. I didn't want to disappoint her or worry her. Besides, she was so sick. In fact, the day I bought the pregnancy test was the last day I gave her a bath. She just became too weak to walk to the tub and I wasn't strong enough to carry her, so I gave her a sponge bath every night. I always powdered her to make sure she smelled good afterward.

I did go to the clinic and saw someone there and got vitamins and tried to eat right. I wore baggy tops and jeans and people, especially Tracey Carmichael, whispered that I was getting fat. I wasn't sure what I was going to do about the baby, so I just didn't think about it. It was easier that way. I concentrated on taking care of Grandma, who grew weaker by the day.

As the days came and went, I fell into a deep depression. Everyone I had ever loved had left me. Grandma insisted on talking about my future without her. She discussed her will and money and what kind of service she wanted and I couldn't bear to listen.

I juggled caring for her and going to school, although it seemed I spent more time at home than in school as Grandma got worse. I only needed two classes to graduate and my adviser helped me arrange to have them in the morning so I could take care of Grandma the rest of the day. I stopped working at the grocery store, too.

I don't know what I would have done if I wouldn't have been able to drive. Thank God I got my license as soon as I could. I tried to make Grandma's doctor appointments in the afternoon so I wouldn't have to take off school any more than I already was. The pregnancy was just another thing on my growing list of stuff to worry about.

* * *

Lexie stands outside the bathroom. "When you're done, let me know."

"I can't pee if you're standing right there," Olivia yells from the other side of the door.

"OK. I'll wait in my room. Just bring it in when you're done."

Olivia turns on the faucet and goes to the bathroom. By the time she gets back to Lexie's room, a plus sign is already emerging on the test. She hands it to Lexie without looking at it.

Lexie chews her lower lip. "Let's sit on the bed."

"It's bad, isn't it? I'm pregnant. I'm pregnant, aren't I? One freakin' time and I get pregnant. How many other girls do it tons of times and never get pregnant? Oh no. Not me. I do it one time. One time things get a little out of hand and what happens? I end up pregnant. Pregnant! My parents are so going to kill me. Cole's going to hate me. How in the hell am I going to be a dancer when I'll look like an elephant in a leotard? And move like one. Everyone will laugh at me. Make fun of me. My life is ruined. Ruined! Completely! I'd be better off dead. Save my parents the embarrassment."

"Calm down," Lexie says, wrapping her arms around Olivia. "We'll figure things out."

"Figure things out?" Olivia says. "There's nothing to figure out. My life is over."

* * *

I'm overwhelmed by Olivia's feelings – her desperation, anxiety, uncertainty, fear and piercing sadness. I know what she feels, and not just because I can feel what she feels because I'm her moment keeper, but because I experienced what she's experiencing when I was alive. Only it wasn't my first time with Bryan. For me, things got out of control too fast and Bryan and I didn't stop to do what we should have. Still, I was pregnant and didn't want to be.

* * *

I watch as Lexie keeps her arm around a sobbing Olivia, rocking gently side to side, trying to soothe her.

Olivia sniffs. "What do I tell Cole?'

"The truth," Lexie says.

"But what if he hates me?"

"He's not going to hate you."

"My parents will hate me."

"They're not going to hate you either. Cole loves you; they love you."

"Maybe I don't have to tell them. I can keep it a secret."

Lexie stops rocking and pulls her arm from around Olivia, using both hands to turn Olivia so Olivia is facing her. "You do have options."

"Like what?"

"Like you don't have to have the baby. A girl in my old school left on a Friday pregnant and when she returned Monday she wasn't anymore."

"I could never do that."

"OK. You could have the baby and put it up for adoption. You were adopted. So was I, and look at the great families we ended up with."

"True. But I could never give up my baby. What kind of mother could do such a thing?"

"My mother did. Yours, too."

Olivia starts crying harder.

"I didn't mean that like it sounded. What I meant is that there are lots of teens who get pregnant and give their babies away because they're not ready to be a parent. The adopting family gets the baby they've always wanted and the pregnancy doesn't stop the teen from going to college or..."

"Be a dancer," Olivia says.

"Or that. I'm not saying that's what you should do. All I'm saying is that you do have options."

* * *

Unlike Olivia, I had no one to confide in when I realized I was pregnant. On top of it, I had to take care of Grandma, who I was bathing and spoon-feeding in an attempt to get her to eat. I struggled in school, and I struggled at home. Nothing in my life was easy or happy. And, well, after Grandma died, I didn't see any reason to live. And yet, I had hoped to save my baby.

I could have waited until after it was born. I thought about it. A lot. But then one night after Grandma died and I hadn't left the house in a week, most of which I spent in bed sleeping, I just did it. Researched it. Planned it. And prayed. I don't know if my baby survived. I hope he did. I say "he" because I always imagined it was a boy. I pictured a little Bryan, with red hair and a dimple in his chin.

***

Olivia calls Cole. "Can we talk?"

"Sure. What's up?"

"Can you come over?"

"I thought you were spending the night with Lexie."

"Change of plans," Olivia says.

"I'll be right there."

"Can you pick me up at Lexie's?"

"Uh, sure. Now?"

"Yeah."

Olivia pushes the off button on the phone. "He's coming over."

"Good, now remember what we talked about," Lexie says.

Olivia nods her head, and the tears begin again.

Lexie slips her arm around Olivia.

"It's just that, we talked about it afterward," Olivia says. "You know, after we did it. And we both said it wouldn't happen again until we got some protection. And I was planning to. I even made an appointment at the clinic downtown you told me about. You know how they say you can do it one time and get pregnant? I never believed that. Did you?"

Lexie nods. "I'm going to tell you something that you've got to swear you won't tell a single soul. Pinkie promise. Never ever. I've never told anyone this. And my parents would kill me if they ever found out. There was this one photographer and…"

Olivia blows her nose into a tissue.

Lexie starts anew. "That girl I was talking about at my old school? The one who left on a Friday pregnant and returned on a Monday not pregnant?"

Olivia nods.

"That was me."

Lexie's eyes turn glassy and watery. "And not a day goes by that I don't think about what might have been."

* * *

"You're what?" Cole shifts in the torn car seat, bumping the bush of keys dangling from his steering wheel.

Olivia wanted to talk to Cole some place secluded so they ended up in the overflow parking lot at the mall that is only ever needed at Christmas.

Olivia swallows hard, trying to muster the courage to say it again. Her left eye and thumb twitch. "I'm pregnant."

Cole slams the steering wheel with the palm of his hand. "Shit! Are you sure?"

Olivia shakes she's crying so hard. "I did a pregnancy test."

"At Lexie's?"

"Yeah. She helped me. What are we going to do?"

"Look, Lib. I'm sorry. You know that I love you. But God..."

Cole slams the steering wheel again. "We'll get married. I'll get a job. We'll figure something out. Damn."

"Can you just hold me?" Olivia asks. "Just hold me."

Cole looks at the console separating them and nods toward the back seat. They crawl in the back and Olivia slides next to Cole as he wraps his arms around her and she rests her head on his shoulder.

Cole kisses the top of her head. "We'll figure this out. Promise."

CHAPTER 35

Olivia opens the back door and Daisy is there waiting, her tail wagging as fast as Mrs. Tilley's finger when she's mad at her English class.

Olivia bends down and scoops up Daisy and kisses her black nose. "I love you, too, Daisy girl."

"Is that you, Lib?" her mom calls from upstairs.

"Yeah."

Olivia carries Daisy up to her room, stopping at her parents' bedroom.

"We just had her out so she's good for the night," her dad says.

"Thanks, Dad. Night."

"Isn't it kind of early for you to be going to bed? Everything all right, Lib?" Elizabeth asks.

"It's ten and I'm just tired. Everything's fine. See you in the morning."

Olivia pulls her hair back in a ponytail and showers. She dries off and stands naked in front of her mirror rubbing her hand up and down over her belly button. Then she turns sideways and looks at her flat-as-a-board stomach, wondering what it will look like in nine months.

She slips on the T-shirt Cole gave her, the one he wore the first night they met, and crawls into bed. She always feels closer to him when she wears his shirt. Daisy jumps up beside her and turns around and around before settling next to Olivia, her head on Olivia's stomach. Olivia wonders if Daisy will be jealous of the baby. Then her mind goes on overdrive and she can't stop thinking about dance, the only thing she's ever wanted to do, the one thing she always wanted to be. And the thought of losing it all is too much. Her dreams have been crushed, her life changed forever and the only thing she can do is bury her head into her satin pillow to muffle her thunderous sobs.

Sleep comes eventually, but it doesn't offer much rest. As Olivia's moment keeper, I see her dreams as she's having them. I record those, too.

Olivia's on stage. The spotlight bathes her in a soft white glow. Her back faces the audience. Then she turns around, her graceful arms overhead, and just when she's completely facing the audience she morphs into a giant elephant in a pink tutu. The audience laughs.

Olivia shakes and opens her eyes. She sits up and leans over to check the clock on her nightstand. It's two a.m.

Daisy jumps onto the floor and crawls under the bed to sleep. Olivia goes to the bathroom then crawls back under the satin sheet. She stumbles toward sleep again.

The night continues with one dream after another. The first dream of the night is always the shortest; they get longer and closer together as the night rolls on. It's obvious what's on Olivia's mind.

I never knew until I was a moment keeper how much people dream. We all dream every night. Probably about one dream every ninety minutes. I used to think I didn't dream at all. Now I know I just didn't remember them. Olivia woke directly from the elephant dream, so I'm guessing she'll remember it. When she wakes from a dream, she usually remembers it.

The alarm goes off and Olivia slaps the sleep button. About a half-hour later, her mom walks in. "Getting up for church?"

Olivia moans. "I hardly slept last night. I'm not going."

"Remember that Dad and I are having lunch with the Groves afterward at the club."

"OK. If I'm not here when you get home, I'll probably be at Lexie's."

* * *

When I was pregnant, I had this recurring nightmare. I was asleep in my room and I'd hear a baby crying. I'd go to my dresser where a drawer was pulled out as far as it would go without coming off. A baby nestled in blankets was inside the drawer, which had been made into a bassinet. The baby wanted me to pick him up but I couldn't. Something wouldn't let me. His cries got louder and louder and the only thing I could do was to shut the drawer so I couldn't hear him anymore. So that was what I did. But just as I shut the drawer, a baby hand poked through the thin crack and grabbed my hand and I woke up.

I had that dream a lot. Not sure what it meant, but I bet there's some meaning to it. Maybe it was my unconscious trying to tell me something, but I never figured out what.

* * *

"And just when I turned around and faced the audience I morphed into a huge elephant in a pink tutu," Olivia tells Lexie.

Lexie mashes her lips together. She's trying hard not to laugh, but she loses it. "I'm sorry. I don't mean to laugh. But you turning into an elephant with a pink tutu is over the top."

"Tell me about it. I barely slept last night. If I keep dreaming like this, I won't be able to function."

"It's probably your unconscious playing out your fears. You're obviously upset about how being pregnant will affect dancing."

Olivia nods.

"It'll all work out," Lexie says. "Cole promised he'd stand by you, right?"

Olivia nods.

"And being pregnant doesn't mean you won't be able to dance ever again."

"But it changes everything," Olivia says. "I had so many plans and now I've ruined them all."

* * *

I remember Grandma saying something similar to me, as if it were her fault she got sick.

"Sarah," Grandma said. "Come sit with me for a while."

I moved the red, green, yellow and white webbed lawn chair next to her recliner. I kept the chair in the living room for just this purpose – so I could sit as close to Grandma as possible. I could have carried one of the kitchen chairs into the living room, but this worked just fine.

Grandma's wrinkled hand reached for mine, her hand bones bulging through sun-spotted skin. "I'm sorry I ruined everything."

"Gram, you didn't ruin anything. You can't help you got sick."

Grandma patted my hands. "But maybe if I'd be a better person this..."

I cut her off. I wasn't about to listen to her talk dumb. Sometimes, she'd get into these moods where she said things she knew weren't true. I'm not sure why. Maybe she just needed an excuse.

"Getting cancer wasn't God's way of punishing you for some wrong you might have done," I said. "Besides, you're the kindest, most gentle person I know."

"Did I tell you I want the organist to play 'What a Friend We Have in Jesus'?" she asked.

I nodded. "Yes, that and 'Amazing Grace'."

She squeezes my hand. "Good."

"Do we have to talk about your funeral? Can't we talk about something happy?"

Grandma nods and closes her saggy eyelids, as if she's trying to remember something and picture it in her mind. "Remember that time we went to that Disney ice-skating show?"

"I remember, Gram."

"Saved money in that old coffee can for a year so we could go to that show. Sorry I couldn't afford to take you to Disney World."

"That's OK, Gram. I loved the ice show. I still have the magic souvenir wand you bought me at the show. And the pixie dust you made."

Grandma smiled. "You loved that wand. Always winging it around casting magic spells."

I had forgotten all about that wand and how I pretended to make everyone's dreams come true.

"And remember when you wanted to play the violin?"

"Correction," I said. "You wanted me to play the violin."

Grandma smiled. "Well, you weren't very good at it."

"Gram, I stank."

We both laughed.

"I remember how special you made all of my birthdays, especially my sweet sixteen," I said. "Remember how we went to that fancy hotel downtown and ate in that expensive restaurant that didn't include the prices on the menu?"

Grandma smiled. "Saved a dollar a week for a few years to make that birthday extra special."

"And it was," I said. "We felt like royalty eating in that expensive restaurant with those fancy chandeliers."

Grandma smiles. "I want buried in that floral dress, Sarah. The one I wore that day. Always kept it for special occasions. And meetin' my maker will be the most special day of all."

"Gram," I said. "Can we talk about happy things?"

I sat with Grandma for a while that day, reminiscing about some of our best times together. When I checked on her later, she was dead.

* * *

"But you promised. You promised you'd be there for me," says Olivia, tears exploding from her swollen eyes.

Cole runs his fingers through his dark, curly hair. "I know what I said. But. It's just that I'm supposed to go to college and…"

"So college is more important than me?"

"I didn't say that."

"You didn't have to."

"Look, Lib. I love you. You know that. I'm just not ready for this."

"And I am?"

"I didn't mean it like that. We're both not ready."

"Well, it's a little too late for that realization. You should have thought about that two months ago when you convinced me to have sex with you."

Cole punches the bed and stands up. "Damn it, Lib. That's a cheap shot. You're not going to pin this all on me. You wanted to do it, too. It's not like I forced you."

"Just leave. Leave."

"I don't want to leave you like this. I want to talk about our options."

"Options? There are no options. I'm pregnant. With your child. You don't want it. You've made that clear. Look, this is my problem. Not yours. So just go. Now."

Cole grabs his varsity jacket and takes two steps toward Olivia before she backs away. "Look, Lib. I can't talk to you when you get like this. Can we talk later? When you calm down."

"There's nothing to talk about. We did it once. Once. And I got pregnant and you want out. Well, I'm giving you your out. There's the door."

"Lib, if I could go back in time and change that one moment I would." Cole walks out the bedroom door and Olivia throws one of Daisy's squeaky toys at him. The rubber bone hits Cole in the back but he doesn't turn around.

Olivia flops on her bed and pulls her boney knees up to her heaving chest. She and Cole have never fought that badly before and she feels guilty because she knows he's right: it was a cheap shot. It wasn't his fault any more than it was her fault.

She spots her purple fuzzy bathrobe draped over the footboard of her cherry bed. She pulls the belt out and sits up, wrapping it around her right hand. She's thinking about killing herself, about using her bathrobe belt, wondering if it's strong enough or if she should use one of the leather belts in her closet. She's never thought such horrible thoughts before, but she doesn't know if she can face this alone or hurt her parents so badly.

She slams the bed with her fist. She doesn't understand why Cole changed his mind. Last night, he promised he would be there for her. Today, he's having second thoughts.

Olivia wonders how long her parents will be gone. They called after their luncheon with the Groves and asked if Olivia minded if they went with the Groves to some art festival. Said they wouldn't be home until late. So after Olivia got home from Lexie's and Cole called and said he had to talk to her right away, she told him to come over.

Cole told Olivia that his parents asked what colleges he wanted to visit before he made his final college decision so they could plan their work schedules around the visitations. He said he kept thinking about how to tell them that he wasn't going to college. That their dream of him being the first one in their family to get a college education just went up in smoke because he got careless and did something stupid. And how he just couldn't disappoint them like that. Couldn't they figure something out, something that would allow him to go to college and Olivia to do the same in a year?

Olivia's cell phone rings. It's Lexie. Olivia doesn't answer it. She doesn't feel like talking to anyone – not even Lexie. She goes to the kitchen to get a drink and as she pulls the tab on her Diet Pepsi she notices the knife block in the corner of the counter. She walks over to it and pulls a knife out. She examines it and thinks how easy it would be to run it over her wrist. But just as quickly as the thought jumps into her mind it goes away. She pushes the knife back in the slot and sits on the couch. Daisy jumps up beside her and rests her head on Olivia's thigh. Her tail slaps the back of the sofa and Olivia runs her hand down Daisy's back.

"I really screwed up this time, girl," Olivia says. "Mom and Dad are going to hate me."

Daisy looks up at Olivia and whimpers.

"I just don't know what to do, Daise. The last thing I want is to hurt Mom and Dad. They always told me that I was the perfect daughter. That we were the perfect family. And what do I do? I screw that up big time. Turns out I'm far from perfect.

"I don't care what people say about me, but I do care what they say about Mom and Dad. Those people at the club, like the Groves, they'll probably gossip and say Mom and Dad have a slut for a daughter. That isn't it a shame that the baby Tom and Liz adopted turned out to be a bad seed. That you never know what you're going to get with one of those adopted babies. After all, they're not blood related. Yep, that's what they'll probably say, Daise."

Olivia stretches out on the sofa. Daisy lies in the crack between Olivia's arm and torso, her head on Olivia's shoulder. Olivia closes her eyes. She's tired, so tired, and she just wants to forget. Sleep sounds good.

CHAPTER 36

"Lib, can we talk?" Elizabeth asks her after school. "You've been moping around the house for a week now. Won't take any of Cole's calls. Don't want to see him when he stops by. What's going on with you two? I've never seen you so down."

"Nothing's wrong," Olivia says. "Except maybe that I don't want to do dance anymore."

Elizabeth drops the jar of mayonnaise she's holding and it hits the tile floor. The glass shatters and goo splatters everywhere.

"Shit!" She turns around and pulls paper towels from the rack behind her while Olivia grabs the dishcloth from the sink.

Olivia kneels down beside her mom and helps clean up the mess. "Sorry, Mom."

Elizabeth looks at her. "Lib, let's clean this up and talk. No buts. No maybe laters. Now. Not wanting to dance when I know that it's all you ever wanted to do tells me there's far more going on in your life that I need to know about."

Olivia rakes her front teeth over her bottom lip and sucks in a breath before parting her lips and releasing it in a heavy sigh. She tries to keep the tears dammed up in her eyes but she's not strong enough. Tears break through and drown her face.

Elizabeth pulls Olivia up by the arm and leads her to the couch. Olivia buries her face into her mom's chest and she sobs like a runaway freight train, full of power and too heavy to stop. Her tears soak the front of her mom's linen blouse.

Elizabeth brushes back Olivia's golden hair and whispers, "It's all right. Everything's gonna be all right. Whatever's wrong we can fix. It'll all work out."

"No, it won't. I've ruined everything. Nothing will ever be all right again."

"Libby," Elizabeth says. "Nothing can be that bad."

"This is. You'll hate me. Dad will hate me. You'll never want to see me again. I should just kill myself."

Elizabeth grabs Olivia's shoulders and straightens her so they are face to face. Olivia's bent head bounces she's crying so hard.

"Look at me," Elizabeth says.

Olivia doesn't lift her head.

Elizabeth puts her hand under Olivia's chin and lifts her head. "Don't you ever, ever say that. You're the best thing that's ever happened to your dad and me. The best thing. And there is nothing, nothing in this world that is so bad that we would never want to see you again."

"I'm pregnant," Olivia heaves. "It was only one time and things got out of hand and Cole says he's not ready to be a dad and I'm not ready to be a mom but I'm gonna be anyhow and I want to dance but now I can't dance and see how I've just ruined my life and your life and Dad's and…"

Elizabeth takes a deep breath and releases a heavy sigh. "I knew it. I just didn't want to believe it. But all of the signs were there. You throwing up in the morning, being more tired than usual. Oh, Lib. I just don't know what to say."

"Say that you love me, that you don't hate me."

"Libby, of course I love you. I could never hate you. Yes, I'm upset. Extremely upset. I thought we had talked about this, had an understanding that when you were ready for this kind of relationship you'd tell me."

"We did," Olivia says. "It just happened so fast and... Oh, Mom, it hurt and there was blood and I feel terrible about it."

Elizabeth hugs Olivia extra tightly. "Everything will be all right, Lib. We'll work things out. When your dad gets home, we'll talk. Yes, I would have preferred this didn't happen until after you finished college and were married, but that's not the way it is. Life doesn't always work out the way we want it to or think it should. But we move on. And moving on might mean changing your dreams, or putting them on hold for a while. But, and this is a very big but, you have your dad and me to help you and support you. We love you and there's nothing we want more than for you to be happy. And sometimes when life hands us unexpected detours, they end up taking us down some pretty awesome roads."

Olivia can't believe her ears. She isn't sure what she expected exactly but she knows it wasn't the love and understanding and support her mom is giving her.

"Will you hold me, Mom?" she asks.

Elizabeth slips her arm around Olivia and Olivia buries her face into her mom's chest once again and they stay like that – for a long time.

* * *

Watching Elizabeth hold Olivia reminds me that no matter how old we are or how independent we think we've become, when we're sick or in trouble or things aren't going as we had planned it's usually our mom that we want most. In my case, it was my grandma.

I wonder if Grandma would have reacted the way Elizabeth did if I had told her I was pregnant. I wonder if I would have chosen a different path if I had told Grandma and she had reacted like Elizabeth. And if Grandma wasn't sick, would things have been different? I have so many questions now that I didn't have then. Then, I felt like Olivia. I thought my life was over. I had lost Grandma. I had lost Bryan. I had no friends, no family – no one. I was all alone in a world that had never been kind to me, except for the parts that Grandma made so.

That was when I remembered Matt's hunting gun. The one Gram kept in her closet. The one she had planned to get rid, just never got around to it.

I had never fired a gun. Wasn't even sure how to put it together. But I figured it out. I thought about my death. I wanted to die but I wanted my baby to live. I thought that if I did it just right and timed it just right, I could accomplish both. So I called 911 and reported a shooting. I waited until the paramedics arrived and just as they walked into the bathroom I pulled the trigger.

* * *

The garage door opens and Daisy jumps off the couch, barks and runs to the back door. She knows the sound of Tom's car pulling into the garage and waits for him by the door that leads to the garage. Her barking wakes up Elizabeth and Olivia.

Olivia sits up; her left eye and thumb are twitching. "I'm afraid to tell Dad."

"I'll be with you. And I think Dad and I have some things we ought to tell you, things we've been waiting until you were old enough to understand. Now seems like the right time."

Elizabeth's remarks puzzle Olivia. She has no clue what her mother is talking about.

As Tom walks into the kitchen he sees what's left of the mess. Elizabeth and Olivia walk in.

"You two look like you just woke up." He nods at the broken glass and mayonnaise. "What happened?"

"Stupid me dropped a jar of mayonnaise and, well, Libby and I had to talk so I didn't get it all cleaned up."

"Talk?" Tom looks at Elizabeth, then Olivia. "Must have been important."

"It was," Elizabeth says.

"Do I get to know, or is it mother/daughter stuff?"

Elizabeth looks at Olivia. "It's family stuff, but let's clean up this mess before Daisy drags mayonnaise all over the house."

Tom gets the sweeper to pick up the glass and Olivia gets the mop and bucket. Elizabeth wipes off the cabinets and counter. When they're done they go into the living room.

"Everything all right, Liz? You two are scaring me."

Elizabeth looks at Olivia and nods.

Olivia wants to be the one to tell her dad but every time she tries to speak, the words get tangled on her tongue and she can't untangle them and get them to come out.

Tom looks at her. His dark eyes search her green for some kind of hint. "What's wrong, Lib? You can tell me. You know you can tell me anything."

"And you won't hate me?"

"Hate you? Never. I love you. Now what's all this about?"

The floodgates open and Tom sits on the leather chair as he's hit by an avalanche of words he never saw coming. As the words gather speed they roll over him, burying him in a blanket of disappointment so thick he can barely move.

"And we only did it one time but I got pregnant just from that one time and I really wish I could go back and make another choice but I can't and I don't want you to hate me but you probably do and I wouldn't blame you if you did because I screwed up your and mom's life and—"

"Stop!" Tom stands and walks over to where Olivia sits and squeezes in beside her. He hugs her as tightly as he can without hurting her and she collapses into his thick arms. Tears zig-zag down Tom's cheeks and he glances at Elizabeth, who's sitting on the other side of Olivia. She's crying, too.

"Look, Lib," says Tom, kissing the top of her head. "I love you. Yes. I'm not happy. A part of me is mad as hell. If Cole were here I'd probably have him up against that wall." He nods at the wall.

"But it's not just Cole's fault," Olivia says. "It's mine, too."

Tom sighs. "Yeah. I know. But I'm still mad at him. I can't help it. But you both were stupid, really stupid. How many times have we talked about this? How many times have we told you that if and when you were ready for this kind of thing that you'd come talk to us?"

"I know," Olivia sobs. "I screwed up and I'm sorry."

Tom looks at Elizabeth. "But I love you and your mom and I will help you get through this. It's not going to be easy, but we'll work things out."

"I think it's probably time to tell Olivia about her birth," Elizabeth says. "And I think we should give her the stuff her mother left her."

Tom runs his fingers through his graying hair. "Look, Liz. I'm just not sure if now's the right time."

Elizabeth clears her throat. "Olivia told me that she thought about killing herself. She was so worried about hurting and embarrassing us that she didn't know what else to do."

Tom's eyes widen. "Is that true, Lib? That thought actually crossed your mind?"

Olivia nods. "I didn't think you and Mom would want me anymore."

"Want you?" Tom hugs her again. "We love you, Lib. Not because you're a great dancer or because you get good grades but because you're you. Don't you know that life is too precious to ever think that way? I've spent my entire life trying to save people. I saved you."

Olivia doesn't quite understand what her dad means by saving her. If he means he saved her by adopting her, providing her with a good home and a loving family. Or if he means he physically saved her and she was just too young to remember it. Since she's allergic to bee stings, she figures it was probably the first time she got stung, before they knew how deadly a bee sting could be to her.

* * *

As I watch this moment unfold, I'm struck by the deep love they have for one another. And I think about Olivia's birth mother and wonder if she knows what an incredible daughter she had. I wonder where she is now, what became of her and if she somehow knows that her daughter was blessed with this wonderful family.

Like Olivia's birth mother, I left some things for my baby. One of the things was a letter I had written the night before I killed myself. I was never good at expressing myself, and I worried that I wouldn't be able to put into words what I felt. I wanted my baby to know how sorry I was for not being strong enough and how sorry I was that I would not be around to see him grow up. I always wondered about that letter and about the forgiveness I had asked for.

* * *

"What about Cole?" Tom asks. "How's he dealing with all this?"

Olivia sighs. "Not well. At first, he was all supportive but then his parents started planning college visits and he started to freak out. And we had a big fight, the worst ever, and I've pretty much ignored him since."

"Do you love him?" Tom asks.

Olivia nods. "But I know that we're young and that we screwed up."

"Does Cole want to go to college?" Tom asks.

Olivia nods again. "Yeah, but I guess now he thinks he can't."

"What do you want?"

Olivia looks down at the floor. She's been thinking about this since she learned she was pregnant. Her mind's been on overdrive. Giving the baby up for adoption is an option she's considered, but she just can't bring herself to do that. Still, she knows she needs help and wants Cole to go to school and would still like to go to school herself. Maybe be a dance teacher, open her own studio one day. So she tells her parents all of this and waits for their reaction.

Tom looks at Elizabeth and she gives him a nod of approval. They've been together so long that she knows what he's thinking and agrees with what he's going to say.

"If you let us, your mom and I will raise the baby. You'll always be his or her mother, but we'll help to provide a loving home, one that will allow you and Cole to continue your education. That is, if that's OK with you and, of course, Cole."

Olivia's eyes are as big and bright as headlights. Again, the words get tangled on her tongue and she can't get them untangled enough to make them come out straight.

"You don't have to say anything now," Tom says. "Course we'll have to talk to Cole, too. And there's something else I want you to know about. Something important I've been waiting your whole life to share with you. It's about the day you were born."

Tom looks at Elizabeth and she leaves and returns with a plastic, brown storage bin. She pulls the leather hassock in front of the couch where Tom and Olivia sit and they join hands so that Olivia is holding both of her parents' hands and Tom and Elizabeth are holding hands. A perfect triangle that will never be broken.

Tom clears his throat. "A day hasn't passed that I haven't thought about the day you were born. It plays over and over in my mind, every detail etched in my brain forever. You see, Lib, I was there. I delivered you."

Olivia's eyes pop. Never in a million years would she have guessed that her adoptive dad had actually delivered her.

Elizabeth squeezes Olivia's hand and a tear sneaks out of the corner of Elizabeth's eye, slides down her cheek and slips into her mouth.

"You know, Lib," Tom says, "life can be crazy. Sometimes we're put in a certain place at a certain time for a certain reason and we just don't see the why right away. That's what happened to me the day you were born. I had finished working at the hospital and decided to take the long way home, something I had never done before. I was always in a hurry to get home to your mom, but on this particular day, for some odd reason, I had an urge to take the longer route. On my way home, I saw an ambulance pull in front of an apartment building and I had this feeling that I should stop, see if I could help. But I ignored the thought because I wanted to get home to your mom. And just as I passed the ambulance, the car radio, which was turned off, screamed in my ears. The windshield wipers, also turned off, flicked as fast as they could. The four-way blinkers started to flash and the horn sounded. I've never been a real praying man, but I knew the guy upstairs was trying to get my attention. So I pulled over and ran as fast as I could up the street to where the ambulance was parked. I sprinted up the steps and entered the apartment a few steps behind the paramedics."

* * *

Omigod! Omigod! Omigod! This can't be happening. This can't be for real. I remember that day. This is my death. This is my moment. And Tom's moment. And Olivia's moment. I feel like I'm going to suffocate. I never saw this coming. Never. I knew there were three men, but I never got a good look at the guy standing behind the paramedics; he arrived a few seconds after the paramedics got there.

I was in the bathroom, holding the gun I found in Gram's closet, the one she never got around to getting rid of. I yelled for the paramedics to come into the bathroom and when they came around the corner and opened the door, I told them that I was pregnant, and to please save my baby. Then I pulled the trigger and thudded to the floor, sinking in a pool of blood.

* * *

"So what happened?" Olivia asks, tears streaking her face once again.

"Are you sure you want to hear this?" Tom asks.

Olivia nods.

"The girl called out that she was in the bathroom. When we got there, she said that she was pregnant. She asked us to save her baby. Then she shot herself and fell to the floor. I'll never forget there was an Ace of Hearts lying in the pool of blood. I pushed through the paramedics, told them that I was a doctor and that I could perform a C-section. And I did. I got you out of your mother's womb as quickly as I could. Your mother didn't live long enough to hear your cry."

Tom and Elizabeth and Olivia are crying, no longer holding hands but hugging one another all at once.

* * *

I can't move. I can't begin to explain what I'm feeling. To realize that the child I have been keeping moments for this entire time was my baby. To realize how close Olivia was to making the same mistake I had made but by the grace of God was saved by a loving and supportive family, the kind of family I had prayed my child would find. And I thank the matchmaker for assigning me to Olivia, for allowing me to be a part of her life and for giving me the peace I never had while living.

I'm so overwhelmed that while I keep recording this moment I can't help but remember all the others that preceded it. They wash over me, from the day Olivia was named to the day she gave herself to Cole. And then I notice, really notice, how much we look like one another. I hadn't seen it before, probably because I wasn't looking for it. And probably because I always envisioned that my baby was a boy and that he looked like Bryan. But now I see it so clearly that I don't know why it took an earthquake of a revelation to shake some sense into me. The blonde hair, green eyes and dimples – just like me.

* * *

"There's more," Elizabeth says. "Your dad found this."

Elizabeth opens the brown bin and takes out a white shoe box with a size seven sticker on the side. "For my baby" is printed in black marker on top.

Olivia opens the box and takes out a letter – the letter I wrote. She reads it out loud.

Baby,
I'm sorry I wasn't strong enough. I'm sorry that I won't be here to watch you grow up. Too many bad things happened to me that I could never explain in a letter, but I want you to know that you were not one of them. I loved your father. He was the only man I ever loved. I hope that if all goes as I've planned, you will live and have a wonderful life and be raised by a family who loves and cares for you in ways I never would have been able to. I could never be the mother you deserve or give you the life that you deserve. I hope that someday you will be able to forgive me.
Love, Mom

Olivia closes her eyes and whispers, "I forgive you, Mom."

Olivia finds the heart pendant Bryan had given me and the Ace of Hearts Tom had retrieved from the pool of blood. Then she lifts out the black Bible and runs her thin fingers over my name embossed in gold on the front. "My mom's name was Sarah," Olivia sobs. She flips through the Bible and finds the red carnation tucked between pages at first Corinthians, chapter thirteen, verse thirteen. She reads the verse that I highlighted in pink so many years ago. "And now these three remain: faith, hope and love. But the greatest of these is love."

The last thing she finds is a faded fortune – wrinkled, torn and taped. She reads it out loud. "Your dreams will come true."

And for the first time in a long time, Olivia has hope that they will.

* * *

I want to do something to show Olivia and Tom and Elizabeth that I'm there, so I focus on surrounding them in a blanket of warmth. I concentrate on wrapping them in my energy and hold it as long as I can.

They glance in my direction all at once and I see their surprised looks and I know that they feel my presence. That they know that I'm there.

"Do you see that?" Olivia asks. "That sort of glow over there."

Elizabeth and Tom don't take their eyes off of where I stand. "Yeah," they say in unison. "We see it."

And I know that it's me they're talking about. That it's me they feel. That it's a moment they will never forget. And neither will I.

7 months later

Cole bends down to tie his shoe and spots a dime heads up on the parking lot at the club. He picks it up and slips it into his pocket. They are going to dinner to celebrate Cole's graduation and acceptance into the local university. The past seven months have been a tornado of action, from dealing with Cole's pissed off parents — who refused to join them for dinner — to Olivia coming to terms with her future in dance.

To be honest, the moments haven't all been happy. Some have been extremely difficult and challenging. Others heartbreaking.

There's Cole's acceptance that he doesn't have his parents' blessing and probably never will. They can't get past their anger even though he's going to college, just as they'd always hoped he would, to study medicine. He wants to be a doctor like Tom.

Olivia has had to rethink her plans too, but she finally feels good about her new path. She plans to earn a bachelor of arts in dance education and hopes to open a dance studio one day. Both she and Tom can get their degrees locally while living with Olivia's parents, who will help with the baby.

Olivia's year has been full of whispers behind her back, people pointing when they think she isn't looking and judging her without knowing anything about the situation. But she's been strong and has discovered that true friends, like Lexie, don't abandon you.

Tom and Elizabeth have spent the last seven months making plans, turning the spare bedroom into a beautiful nursery for the grandson they can't wait to hold. Now, it's a matter of waiting for that moment when the new little life will join theirs. And me, well, I'm recording the moments, more anxious than ever to meet my grandson for the first time.

* * *

Cole wraps his arm around Olivia as they sit on the couch and touches her belly mountain with his other hand. "Think Zach will like playing baseball?"

Olivia smiles. "Maybe he'll be a dancer."

Cole squirms. "Uh, I'd rather have him play baseball. Or football."

Olivia jabs him with her elbow. "Hey. There are a lot of football players who take ballet in the off season. Helps them maintain their balance, strength and flexibility. So I wouldn't knock it if I were you."

"Maybe, but…"

"Uh!" Olivia sits up. "I felt something."

"Omigod! Is it time? Do you think it's time?" Cole gets up.

Olivia bends over. "Get Mom."

Cole finds Elizabeth and Tom sitting on the patio and when they return Olivia is in a fetal position on the floor and moaning.

Tom examines Olivia while Elizabeth times the contractions.

"I felt water trickle down my leg," Olivia says.

"Is she going to be all right?" Cole asks.

"Get the bag, Cole. We're going to the hospital."

* * *

I've never been so afraid for Olivia. I know she's in a lot of pain because I feel it, too. I remember how my mother died giving birth to me and I pray that God will bring Olivia through childbirth and that her son will be healthy.

"Can't we just go through the red light if there's no one at the intersection?" Cole asks. He's sitting in the backseat with Olivia and she's doubled over in pain. "If a cop stops us, we can just tell him we're having a baby."

Tom glances back at Olivia, looks every way to make sure no cars are coming, then puts his four-way flashers on and speeds through the red light. When they get to the hospital, Olivia is whisked away and the moments come so fast I have to really focus on capturing them and not getting distracted.

"When I say 'push', Olivia, push," the doctor says.

Elizabeth is on one side of Olivia and Cole is on the other.

Tears stream down Cole's face. "I'm so sorry, Lib. So sorry I put you through this."

Olivia looks at him and manages a smile. "Go ahead. Watch your son being born."

Cole kisses her hand and goes down to the end of the bed.

"Now, push!" the doctor says.

"I see his head, Lib. He's almost here," Cole says.

Elizabeth squeezes Olivia's hand and I send all the energy I can, wrapping them in love and warmth.

"Push," the doctor says again. "Just one more big push and that's all we need."

Olivia bears down and pushes as hard as she can and a beautiful bloody body with ten fingers and toes — none of them webbed — slides out into the doctor's waiting arms.

"Is he all right?" Olivia cries.

"He's perfect, Lib," says Cole as he cuts the umbilical cord.

It's then that I notice the strawberry-blond hair glued to his tiny head and I wonder.

I feel him before I see him. Bryan's beside the baby, looking down. A loving warmth radiates from his moment-keeper body. And I know that he didn't abandon me. That there was no way for him to reach me – until now.